"**W**hen was the last time you really looked at the buildings in town—really appreciated them for their architecture?" Amanda asked.

"Hmmm . . . that would be never."

"Exactly." She laughed. "'To see what is in front of one's nose needs a constant struggle.'" She pointed out a snakelike figure carved above the door of the bank, informing me that the buildings with the bowl-and-serpent markings were once owned by the Orion College of Pharmaceuticals and used for various administrative offices and student housing.

"And now they're being used for places like banks and bakeries," I said.

"But things aren't always as they appear."

"Meaning?"

"Meaning there's more to the markings than meets the eye. Symbols and codes aren't at all accidental. Everything has a purpose."

the AMANDA project

Shattered

BOOK THREE
BY AMANDA VALENTINO
AND LAURIE FARIA STOLARZ

An Imprint of HarperCollinsPublishers

FOURTH STORY MEDIA
NEW YORK

HarperTeen is an imprint of HarperCollins Publishers.
Shattered
Text copyright © 2012 by Fourth Story Media
Illustrations copyright © 2012 by Fourth Story Media

Fourth Story Media

Fourth Story Media, 115 South Street, 4F, New York, NY 10038

www.epicreads.com

Library of Congress Cataloging-in-Publication Data is available
ISBN 978-0-06-174217-0

Book design by Polly Kanevsky and Dale Robbins
11 12 13 14 15   LP/BV   10 9 8 7 6 5 4 3 2 1

First Edition

Alex and Talia
A Special Note of Thanks

Nia and I would like to give special thanks to Alex and Talia Grimaldi, the owners of Caffe Luna in Orion, Maryland. Nia and I loved meeting at your cozy café to discuss <u>Shattered</u>: to review chapters, get our facts straight, and go over details and edits. We greatly appreciated your hospitality and kindness: all the times you opened early for us and stayed late; for always having the very best espresso (for me) and café mocha (for Nia); and for all the tasty treats. Alex, the vegan anise-and-apricot biscotti was simply amazing—thanks so much for altering your recipe just for me. And Nia swears by your pignoli nut macaroons. Now that the book is finished, we'll certainly miss our time spent with both of you, but Nia promises to stop by at least once a week, and I'll be sure to come visit the very next time I'm in town.

Big hugs to you both,
Laurie Stolarz & Nia Rivera

"Life is partly what we make it,
and partly what it is made by the friends we choose."

—Tennessee Williams

the AMANDA project
Shattered

CHAPTER 1

Once upon a time, there was a girl named Amanda, the physical and emotional equivalent of a glass of sparkling champagne. And one day, Amanda dropped into Nia's life, jumbled it around, shimmered it up, and forced her to look at life from a totally new perspective. Then Amanda disappeared without a word. And Nia's fairy tale turned into a nightmare.

Hello, faithful readers, Nia here. It's finally my turn to take over. Not that I don't trust Hal's and Callie's accounts, but we all know who is really on top of things around here. I thought I would start off with the above. Because it explains exactly what Amanda did: She took my life, upended it, and vanished. To be fair, she did leave me with friends I never expected to have and, well, a ME

I never expected to be either, but that is what I intend to tell you about.

Now, to our developing story . . .

Location: My room

Players: Hal, Callie, and me. And some surprise characters.

Time: 4:30 P.M. Tuesday.

Hal and Callie were there, in my deep purple hideaway that my mother had carefully decorated with framed posters of movie goddesses and freedom fighters of the mid-twentieth century. My heroes. This gathering would have been unthinkable only weeks before—the loner artist and the former I-Girl spending time with the ultimate outcast? But Amanda had changed all that. Because Amanda had asked them to be her guides, too.

At the moment, her guides were pondering the crumbs she had left for us, a rich and creamy nougat-filled Pandora's box of mystery—a glossy, black-buttoned coffer, recently liberated from the House of Bragg, much the worse for wear.

"Check this out." Callie laughed, flashing us a photo of what appeared to be Amanda, around age five, dressed in a pixie costume for Halloween.

The photo was from Amanda's box.

We'd unearthed the box among Amanda's other belongings at Play It Again, Sam's, a thrift shop downtown. The owner was an impressively imposing, almost

Delphic woman named Louise. Louise had steered us toward the box, but refused any elaboration.

Initially the box had been nearly impossible to open, but finally, working together, we were able to push its mysterious buttons in precisely the right way . . . and we were in. Today was only our second opportunity to scrutinize the contents. The first time had been rather rushed—only enough time to be tantalized.

The box was full of Amanda puzzle pieces of all sorts—pieces that made little sense on their own, but perhaps all together would start to form a clearer picture.

We also found a congratulations-on-your-recent-addition-to-the-family card from someone named Dr. Joy (apparently the same someone who signed our vice principal out of the hospital after he'd been attacked in his office); the death certificate of a woman named Annie Beckendorf; and a custody document placing Annie's younger daughter under the guardianship of Annie's older daughter, Robin Beckendorf (what had happened to the father was a complete mystery to us).

After seeing the words "Beckendorf Girls" written on the back of a photo with a woman and an older and younger girl—we had deduced that Amanda was the minor listed in the custody document; that Annie Beckendorf must have been Amanda's mother; and that after Annie's death, Amanda's older sister, Robin, had gotten legal custody of Amanda.

A stark contrast to all the familial tales she'd told us.

But, at this point, how could we really be surprised?

As if things couldn't get any more perplexing, flipping through the photos, we came across one that had the people's heads cut out. My first thought: morbid, possibly even sadistic . . . but no—never, not Amanda. Maybe she'd pasted the heads someplace else, like in a collage, or an art installation, or even in a locket, perhaps.

The box also held a plethora of bizarre collectibles: a pouch of scented dirt; old airline and bus tickets for places like Denver and Washington, D.C.; tourism brochures for the town of Orion; as well as an old hospital bracelet that someone had doubled up, possibly to wear like a ring.

It was all very puzzling indeed. But one thing was clear: These items must have been important to Amanda because she'd enshrined them in the box and kept them as she migrated across the country.

Right?

We hadn't kept the box stashed at my house for fear that my fastidiously neat mother would find it in my closet. But since my mother had been so preoccupied organizing an auction event at our church, and we needed someplace safe to keep it (our house has a security system), my closet seemed to be relatively safe territory, particularly the area behind my towering collection of Encyclopedia Britannicas.

"Whoa," Callie said, holding up a photo of a thirteen-year-old Amanda getting baptized in a lake. "I didn't even know Amanda was religious."

"She's not," Hal said. "She told me that she was raised Unitarian, that her parents didn't believe in looking for answers to all of life's mysteries, but to explore those mysteries from different perspectives." He smiled at his own memory. "Somehow it's not hard to remember what Amanda says. Why doesn't it work that way with teachers?"

I chewed my thumbnail down to the quick (much to my French-manicured mother's chagrin), remembering that Amanda had told me she'd been looking for a Catholic church to continue her confirmation studies, and I'd suggested she join mine. "In other words, she was lying," I said, glaring.

"There's a surprise." Callie rolled her eyes.

In some respects, it was odd to think of Amanda as a liar. She always seemed so resolute about everything, like there was never any reason to doubt her for a moment. And yet, ever since I'd met Hal and Callie, it felt like I was doing nothing but.

The crazy thing—as if finding your friend's belongings in a thrift store after she disappears isn't crazy enough—was that we had just gotten the box back after it had been stolen from Hal. Heidi Bragg, leader of the I-Girl pack and one of the most popular girls at Endeavor High School, had batted her eyelashes at Hal and snatched it right out from under his nose. No sour grapes here; that is exactly what happened, almost like she'd hypnotized him with her charm—boom, box gone. The fact that the box was now dented and scratched suggested that Heidi and/or her mother had tried and failed to get inside.

Fortunately, we managed to locate the box in Mrs. Bragg's secret home office during the post-play cast party. It was sitting on a chair not far from vials of disturbing blood samples. The whole situation seemed increasingly diabolical.

While Callie and Hal continued to sort through Amanda's box, I reached for the book on my bedside table, knowing that it was about time I made my own confession. I'd found the book under my pillow, left for me by Amanda shortly after she'd gone missing—but I had never told Hal and Callie about it.

Wrapped in layers of silver wax paper, it was a first-edition copy of Sylvia Plath's *Ariel*. I took a deep breath, confident that the book was a message, and replayed in my mind the first time I met Amanda.

It was in the rare books room of the library; I had been trying to get away. From time to time I escaped from everyone and everything, sitting at the way back behind the stacks, to lose myself. There was something both comforting and enthralling about all those old, well-worn books with their tattered pages and well-kept secrets. It was the closest thing I'd found to pushing the pause button on my life.

So, there I was, minding my own business, when this girl

walked in. "Well, hello there," she said right away, somehow spotting me despite the fact that I was partially—though strategically—obscured by a large marble column. A mysterious smile stretched across her heart-shaped face, as if she couldn't have been happier with the world, while I, on the other hand, for more reasons than I could possibly list, couldn't have been more irritated by it.

"Hi," I muttered back, noticing right away the dress that she was wearing. Her whole look was straight out of a 1920s black-and-white movie, something starring Rudolph Valentino or Greta Garbo. The dress was sleek and simple on top, but very flapper-girl-esque at the bottom the way it bellowed out. Her hair was bobbed and jet-black with blunt-cut bangs, circa 1926.

She made a beeline to the rarest of the books, kept under lock and key only a few feet away from me. "*Ariel* by Sylvia Plath," she purred. "Palpably powerful, don't you think? They say that poets are the nurturers of the soul. Would you agree?" She pointed to a copy behind the glass.

I looked around to make sure she was talking to me, that she wasn't simply murmuring to herself. And then I shrugged, definitely intrigued, because it wasn't every day—or even every year—that another student piqued my interest, at least as far as anything literary goes. "I haven't read it," I confessed, feeling my face turn pink. I wondered how I could possibly have missed it.

"Really?" She cocked her head. "These were some of the

last poems that Sylvia ever penned . . ."

"I know," I said, fully aware of the history, since I'd practically memorized most of Plath's other work. Had I been spending too much time reading the works of Chaucer and Baudelaire? James Joyce and Henry James? Jean-Paul Sartre and Pablo Neruda? Had my temporary obsession with the Romantics and Victorians—Jane Austen, George Eliot, Oscar Wilde—kept me away? Or perhaps (embarrassing as it is to admit), it was my slightly longer detour with the Beat poets?

"I'm Amanda, by the way." She turned to me, perhaps waiting for me to get up and shake her hand, but instead I remained firmly in place.

"Nia," I said, finally.

"Nice name. You know that it means 'radiance' in Gaelic, don't you?"

"As well as Welsh." I nodded. "And 'purpose.' My mother finds that appropriate."

Amanda scratched her chin, as if in thought, which is when I noticed the dark brown mole on her upper lip. I wondered if it was fake, if her whole look might indeed be fake.

"Is there a party somewhere?" I asked, gesturing at her outfit, not intending for it to come out rude—but then again, not really caring if it did. Luckily Amanda didn't take it that way. She simply tilted her head, as if confused by the question. "Funny that you would ask that . . ."

"Right," I said again, making an attempt to put my nose back into Sartre's *No Exit*, the original French version.

"So, this was Anne Sexton's copy of *Ariel*?" she continued, turning back to the book, still talking to me.

Finally I got up to join her. I was enthralled to see—
though angry at myself for missing it before—all that I had
been missing by sitting at the back of the room.

"Anne and Sylvia went to school together," Amanda whispered, her intimacy contagious. "They were both rebel-poets
with serious depression issues."

"And they both ended up killing themselves," I added
solemnly.

"Tragically fascinating, isn't it?" Her black-lined eyes grew
wide. "So, do you suppose that if we inquire at the desk, the
librarian will let us see the actual pages? Because I've heard
that Anne's notes are scribbled in the margins."

"They would never let us—" I started to answer, but
Amanda cut me off.

"Never hurts to try," she interrupted, holding up a bejew-
eled finger.

I couldn't help but take her whole look in: the glitter sprinkled over her cheeks, the antique silver key around her neck,
and the pretty purple pumps that matched the feather clipped
to her headband. I glanced down at the layers of darkness
draped over my body: an old, baggy T-shirt, pants so long
that the hems got caught beneath the heels of my shoes, and
an all-weather trench coat.

I was surprised by all she knew, and by how much we
seemed to have in common despite how obviously different
we appeared. We ended up standing there for a good hour
that day in front of the glass cabinet, never moving from it,

9

comparing insider information about famous dead poets and our shared love of classic movies and vintage sound tracks. I discovered that Amanda had recently moved to Orion, and that we'd be going to school together at Endeavor High.

It was then that she asked me to be her guide.

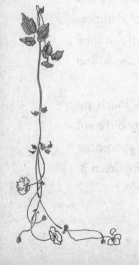

CHAPTER 2

I opened the *Ariel* cover, mindful that I hadn't really handled the book much—perhaps just a couple of times since I'd found it—mostly because I knew how valuable it was. Shortly after I had received it, I went to the library, borrowed a copy, and read through the poems at least a dozen times.

What Amanda had told me about the collection was true: It was stunning. I mean, really stunning: "Stasis in darkness. / Then the substanceless blue / Pour of tor and distances. . . ."

How was it that I'd never read these lines before? And yet, as beautiful as they were, I still didn't have any answers.

While Hal and Callie kept busy sorting through Amanda's precious belongings, I thumbed through the first few pages of *Ariel*, knowing that a first-edition copy must have cost Amanda a fortune, and wondering how she possibly could have afforded it.

I closed my eyes and tried to imagine where she bought it. An old bookshop? A random yard sale? EBay? But for some reason I pictured a small antique shop that sold knickknacks as well as books, and a tiny, frail man at the front desk, ringing up orders using a calculator and a notepad rather than a cash register or a credit card scanner like everybody else.

In my mind's eye, I could see this man handing the book to Amanda without so much as a bag, despite its value. I then flashed to a scene earlier in its history: being passed around a group of girls, all dressed the same in 1960s plaid bib jumpers, probably from a prep school.

I dropped the book and opened my eyes, my brain whirling with questions. Those visions had been so intense . . . so specific. "This is all too peculiar." I exhaled.

"Well, peculiar or not, it's not like we have any other choice but to piece this stuff together," Callie said. "How else are we going to find Amanda?"

"Hey, are you expecting someone, Nia?" Hal asked from the window seat.

A second later the doorbell rang. Jumping up, Hal grabbed the duvet off my bed to conceal the contents of Amanda's box. Meanwhile, I got up and opened my bedroom door a crack to listen. My father wasn't home from work yet, and Mama was out at yet another auction meeting, but I'd heard my brother creep in earlier.

I sat crouched at the top of the stairs, looking down as Cisco emerged from the family room. He was rubbing his eyes, as if all that MTV-watching had finally exhausted him. I wondered why he wasn't at soccer practice, and if my parents knew that he'd apparently given himself the day off.

He opened the door to reveal a woman standing on the doorstep. She was probably in her thirties, and I'd never seen her before.

"Who is it?" Hal whispered curiously.

I shook my head and tried to listen.

"How can I help you?" Cisco asked.

Minus the magic wand and crown of jewels, the woman looked like someone straight out of a fairy tale. Her golden-blond hair was swept up in a twist. Her face was like a porcelain doll's, with starry blue eyes and angular cheeks, and she was wearing a long pink coat that at first glance looked more like a dress.

"I need to speak to Nia Rivera," the woman said, peering beyond Cisco into our house. She reminded me of a 1950s movie star, which I thought was sort of intriguing, because the first time I'd met Amanda, she made me think of the movies, too. "Who is it?" Hal repeated, as if I didn't hear him the first time.

I shushed Hal with one of my usual glares, resisting

the urge to throw something at him. Instead I motioned for him and Callie to come join me at the top of the stairs.

"Is she home?" the woman persisted. "She has something that belongs to me, and I'd really like to retrieve it."

"She isn't home at the moment," Cisco lied, ever the protective older brother, able to detect danger when he sees it. "She's out with some friends."

"Oh?" the woman asked. A tiny but not terribly pleasant smile curled across her seashell lips. "Might those friends be Callista Leary and Hal Bennett?"

Callie and Hal exchanged a look of surprise.

"And you are . . . ?" Cisco asked.

"Forgive my lack of manners." The woman extended her hand to him. "My name is Waverly Valentino. I'm Amanda Valentino's aunt."

Callie let out a gasp, slapping a hand over her mouth.

Meanwhile, Cisco kept a firm grip on the door so the woman couldn't inch her way inside. "How do you know my sister?" he asked evenly, demonstrating his usual near-nauseating charm and unflappable composure.

"I don't, exactly," she explained. "But my niece is missing and I heard that Nia and her friends were looking for her."

"And where did you hear that?"

"The vice principal of their school."

"*Mr. Thornhill?*" Cisco asked, surprise evident in his voice. "When did you talk to him?"

"Just the other day," she said.

"She's lying," Callie whispered, as if it weren't completely obvious. It was no secret that Vice Principal Thornhill had been mysteriously attacked in his office, and therefore unconscious for weeks. More than that, when we tried to visit him at the hospital, we found that he wasn't there. He'd been discharged in the care of a Dr. Joy to a rehab facility.

The woman plucked a tissue from a pink vintage clutch. With a large and floppy leather flower on the front, the purse reminded me of something Amanda might have carried. "Forgive me," Waverly said, blotting her tears with the tissue. "I get really emotional when talking about my niece. What I really need is to get that item back from your sister. I'm sure she won't mind. Maybe you've seen it . . . maybe it's in her room and we could go have a look? I'll only take a moment of your time." She tried to squeeze her way a little farther inside, but Cisco had anticipated her moves.

"I don't think that's possible. I'm sorry I can't be more helpful, ma'am," he said.

Sighing, the woman took a card out of her purse. She handed it to Cisco and made him promise to give it to me just as soon as I got home. "All right, young man, if you're sure . . . it's important that you have her call me, otherwise I will have to go to the police."

"I'll let her know. Have a nice day," Cisco said briskly,

doing his best imitation of our father at work, shoving the card into his pocket and closing the door firmly behind her.

I was left with a distinctive chill. Waverly Valentino did not seem like a person to cross.

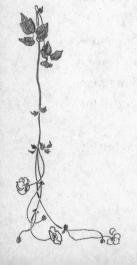

CHAPTER 3

We dashed back to my room and eased my door shut behind us. Hal sprinted to the window again. "No sign of her. She cleared out fast."

"Did Amanda ever mention an aunt to either of you?" I asked them.

Hal shook his head and Callie couldn't seem to remember.

"But she talked about so many different people," Callie admitted, sitting back down on the floor beside the blanket-covered mound of Amanda's box. "Sometimes it was hard to keep up."

I took a seat on the edge of my bed. "She must know we have the box."

"Which means that she's probably connected to Mrs. Bragg somehow," Hal said.

"Why do you think she lied about talking to Thornhill?" Callie asked. "I mean, it doesn't make any sense. Everyone in town knows he's in rehab—somewhere."

"Maybe it's a veiled threat," I guessed. "Or that she wants to get the message across that she knows we have the box."

"My vote," Callie began, "is that her whole story was probably a lie. I'm sure she's not Amanda's aunt, and she's definitely not going to the police either."

"Why *definitely*?" I asked, thinking about Hal's most recent run-in with Orion's (less-than) finest. Officer Nick Marciano had questioned him about Thornhill's attack. But instead of asking all the obvious questions—where Hal was on the night of the attack, if he'd returned to the school or seen anything—the officer seemed far more interested in our search for Amanda.

"Because she's obviously in league with the Braggs," Callie continued.

I shook my head, because nothing seemed obvious to me. "Now that I think of it, maybe this Waverly person *wasn't* lying about Thornhill."

"How could she not have been?" Hal asked, standing by the window, checking to make sure that Waverly was really gone and not lurking somewhere.

"Ever think that maybe she spoke to him someplace else?"

"As in wherever he is?" Callie asked.

"It's possible," I said. "We just can't make any assumptions at this point."

"Agreed," Hal said.

There was a knock on my bedroom door. Without waiting, Cisco invited himself in. Although I just see him as my massively annoying, smotheringly protective older brother, his popularity and good looks are matched by a good nature and kind heart that even I have to admit is admirable. I could see Callie slightly wilting in his presence. He has that effect on girls; the tall-dark-handsome thing is hard to resist. (Why didn't I get at least a little bit of the tall?)

"Care to fill me in?" he asked, handing me Waverly's card.

Her name and phone number were printed across the front in shiny gold lettering. In the bottom right-hand corner was an eye; it looked like a logo. "Wonder what this is." I pointed to the eye.

"I thought that maybe *you* could tell *me*," Cisco said pointedly. "And what's the mysterious item of hers that you supposedly have?"

I bit my lip, surprised at how riled he seemed. My brother was normally super even-tempered.

"I'm not leaving until you spill," he insisted.

"Well, you know that Amanda's missing," Callie said, flustered by Cisco's proximity. She glanced at me; I looked at Hal. Were we going to include him? I felt their approval, and we all relaxed.

"Don't insult me," he said, shifting his big brown eyes to mine.

The whole school knew about Amanda's disappearance, though everyone had their own theories about where she might have gone. Some believed she'd moved to Greece—that her family had purchased a vineyard, and that Amanda was taking Greek lessons by day and stomping grapes at night. Others said that her mother was here illegally—that immigration had finally caught up with her, and now they were all on the run. Less exotic theories existed as well—stories involving the loss of a house, winning the lottery, or a mysterious inheritance. Some didn't even believe she had really disappeared: one girl, Tammi Black, claimed she saw Amanda at Unique, a thrift store just outside of Orion.

No one really knew what to believe.

"It's not exactly privileged information that we're looking for her," I explained.

"It's also not exactly privileged information that you're keeping secrets." Cisco shot me an evil grin. "But I suppose I could always ask Mama and Papi. Maybe *they* might know who that Waverly person was . . . and what you stole of hers."

"And maybe they might also know why you skipped soccer practice today," I volleyed. "I'm sure Papi is really pleased, since he's counting on you to be named MVP for the fourth year in a row."

Soccer at Endeavor was huge and all-important—the team practiced year-round, indoors and outdoors, regardless of the season. Everyone was counting on Cisco to bring the team to Nationals.

"Why don't we start over?" he suggested, calling for a truce.

"Fair enough." I gave a small, satisfied smile, knowing I had won this round.

"We think Amanda might be in serious trouble," Hal started, "but we know she's still out there. I mean, she keeps leaving clues for us."

"Clues?" Cisco's brow furrowed.

"Yes," I said, filling him in on what we had, what we knew, and that a website had been created.

"You may have heard about it?" Hal said. "Theamanda-project.com?"

Cisco gave a subtle nod. "Why doesn't Amanda just call you?"

I rolled my eyes, tired of asking the same question myself. "Apparently, that's not the way she works."

I realized then that I should share my Amanda treasure as well; we needed all of our gray matter on this one. I reached for the copy of *Ariel* again, still mystified by the heart someone had drawn around the title on the front cover. "There's something I have to show you," I said, holding the book out.

"When did you get that?" Hal moved from his window perch to get a better look.

I took a deep breath and told them everything—from my first encounter with Amanda to finding the book under my pillow.

"So there's absolutely no doubt that the book is from her," Hal said.

"But what's with the heart?" Cisco asked.

"I don't know. I don't even know if Amanda was the one who drew it." Part of me assumed that Amanda would never deface something so rare. But another part felt like I didn't know Amanda at all.

"It had to have been Amanda, though. It is so like her." Callie grabbed the hospital bracelet that we'd found in Amanda's box. The bracelet was tiny, from a maternity ward, but it appeared as though someone had tried to make it even smaller by fashioning it into a ring. "Ariel Feckerol," she said, reading the name off the label. "At least I think that's what it says. The type is kind of worn off."

"Wait, *what*?" I asked, completely taken aback by the name, and wondering why I hadn't made the whole Ariel connection when we'd first discussed the bracelet.

"Unless it's a coincidence," Cisco offered, taking the book from me. "I mean, it's possible."

"I don't believe in coincidences." I shook my head. "Especially where Amanda's concerned. She's always so purposeful about everything."

Callie slipped the ring onto her finger, but it fell right off. "This had to have been worn by a man," she said. "I mean, look at the proportion of the radius," she added, referring to the large size.

"A man named Ariel Feckerol?" Hal raised his eyebrow at her.

"What's the date on the bracelet?" I asked.

Callie turned the band sideways to check. "February thirteenth. Fifteen years ago."

"I don't know." Hal sighed, running his fingers through his sandy hair. "Maybe the proof is in the poetry. Maybe there's a verse in that *Ariel* book that'll help make sense of all this."

"I already thought of that," I told them. "But I read the book—practically memorized it—and I couldn't find any clues. It's not as if Amanda stuck a bookmark in a certain page."

"So—why a heart?" Hal grabbed the book from Cisco. "And what took you so long to tell us about this?"

The truth was pretty simple: I hadn't wanted to share the book with anyone. The gift just seemed more special when it was only between Amanda and me.

"As if *you* were completely open with us about going down to Baltimore to see Frieda," I retorted. Frieda was Amanda's artist friend who warned him to stay away from Callie and me because we were in more danger as a trio.

"And, if memory serves," Callie began, tapping her chin, "it seems there might've been something else that you failed to tell us." She was no doubt referring to the pocket watch that Amanda had secretly left for him.

"Point taken." He looked sheepish. Hal ran his fingers over the heart design and a bright pink smear rubbed off on his finger. "Lipstick?" he wondered.

"More like lip liner," Callie corrected. "Lipstick has a smoother finish."

Using the hem of his shirt, Hal proceeded to wipe a corner of the heart away. Within seconds, the bottom V-shaped part was gone.

"There's your answer," Cisco said. "Had to be your friend. No way lipstick could survive in a used bookstore for very long."

Callie nodded. "Amanda must have drawn it."

"*Ariel*," Hal said, reading the title aloud.

I looked down at the business card, wondering if there was any connection between the contents of the box and the woman. Did someone named Ariel work at an eyeglass store, or a place that performed eye exams? "We should call this woman. I doubt that any of what she's saying is actually legitimate, but maybe we'll still be able to get some answers. I don't think we can pass up a lead like this."

"Hold up," Cisco said. "I'm not sure I like the idea of my little sister getting involved in all this—of *any* of you getting involved in it, for that matter. I mean, isn't it bad enough that Thornhill was attacked? Do you honestly want to risk being next?"

"Let's also not forget *when* he was attacked," Hal said. "Shortly after he went to the police to talk about

Amanda's disappearance," Callie whispered.

"Nia?" my mother called from downstairs. "I'm home. Would you like a cup of hot cocoa . . . thick enough to stand your *churros* in?"

"Great," Cisco said, cringing at the fact that our mother was back unexpectedly early from her meeting. He'd either have to confess to skipping practice, or tuck himself away in his room until an opportune time to sneak downstairs as if coming in straight from practice.

"Be down in a second," I called. "Callie and Hal are here, too."

"Absolutely, *pollita*, I'll make plenty," she called back. The understatement of the century. She was pleased I suddenly had friends.

"You still haven't answered my question," Cisco reminded me. "Are you really planning to make yourselves the next victims?"

"What do *you* think?"

"That's why I'm asking, Ni."

"All I'm going to do is call this Waverly woman tomorrow," I said firmly, looking back down at the card, ignoring his big-brotherly concerns. *For now.*

CHAPTER 4

The following day at school, everyone was buzzing about the talent show on Friday.

"I was going to back out of it," Hal said, referring to playing guitar in his boy band Girl Like Me. "Considering everything that's going on with Amanda. But the guys are really counting on me."

"Well, personally, I think it's great," Callie said.

We were in the library during a free period, originally to discuss our impending phone call to Waverly, but we had yet to even broach the topic.

"I mean, Amanda would *want* you to be in the show, don't you think?" Callie continued, giving him one of her dimpled grins.

Hal shrugged, embarrassed by Callie's attention, though he also seemed to enjoy it. I could tell by the way he was smiling, even when he bit his lip, and how pink his face was, like he'd just spent an hour in the sun.

"We should probably get down to business, don't you think?" I asked, trying to shift the focus to the topic at hand.

But they kept carrying on about the talent show—how Hal needed to run to the music shop later; how Callie, having recently declined her I-Girl membership privileges, obviously wouldn't be in the annual I-Girl lip-synch routine.

A tragedy to say the least.

"Are you doing anything, Nia?" Callie asked me.

"Are you serious?" I peeked over at Ms. Wisp, aka Ms. Whisper, the school librarian, who was too busy sorting books to care that we were speaking audibly. "I wasn't even going to go."

"You *have* to go," Hal said. "I've been working on a song for weeks, and I'd really like you to hear it. I want you both to hear it, of course," he corrected himself.

Just then, there was a crash in the corner. It was Zoe Costas, this girl who takes pictures for the school newspaper and plays sax in several bands. She had knocked over a stack of books from a table near us. As Ms. Wisp rushed over to pick them up, I realized that if we ever got back to talking about our search for Amanda, we should be careful about who could overhear our conversation.

Case in point: I heard some loud gum-popping noises behind me and I turned, startled to see Heidi and her

I-Girl clones—I'd thought the library was to them what fast-food restaurants are for my mother: consciously uncharted territory. While Kelli and Traci appeared to be feverishly finishing up some assignment, Heidi shot us a dirty look.

Callie did her best to ignore them by flipping open her French textbook and feigning interest in a picture of *soupe à l'oignon*.

I was just about to broach the topic of the curious eye logo, when I felt someone's hand press down on my shoulder. I turned to look.

Heidi was there.

"Aren't *we* the regular Three Musketeers?" she asked.

I shooed her hand away. "Oooh, up to three syllables today, Heidi—and in a foreign language?"

Heidi rolled her eyes. "I have two reasons for coming to your table," she began, keeping her voice low. "First, I think it goes without saying that Callie's recent social suicide makes her ineligible to lip-synch with us on Friday."

"And as you can see, she's brokenhearted about it," I said, giving Callie a reassuring smile.

"Well, she should be," Heidi said hotly. "Because everyone's been speculating why she continues to hang out with you. At first we thought she was doing some charity work."

"And now?" Callie asked, lifting her chin and making direct eye contact with her.

"Now they simply think you're a charity case, too."

"You mentioned you had two reasons . . . ?" Hal asked pointedly.

"Right." She smiled meanly. "Word is that you're all looking for Amanda. Any luck with that yet? I mean, beyond what's on your lame-o website?"

"It's hardly lame-o," Hal said. "Like you would even care about our search. Everyone knows how much you hate Amanda."

"*Hate* is a strong word."

"But I think it's fairly accurate." He gave her a pointed look.

"Whatever," Heidi said, with a toss of her bottle-blond hair. "So, *have* you guys had any luck?"

"Let me assure you that you are NOT on our need-to-know list," I told her.

"Well, don't look too hard," she said, picking an invisible piece of lint off Hal's sweater. "Endeavor has been a far more peaceful place in Amanda's absence. No more wig-wearing weirdos roaming the hallways with their dime-store junk and ugly trinkets."

"There's no vice principal around either to thwart your quest for power," I said, checking for her reaction.

"Maybe you guys should mind your own business," she snapped.

"And why would we do that?" I asked, encouraged by her anger.

"I think I've wasted enough time here. God knows I

don't want to commit social suicide as well." She stormed off to join Kelli and Traci, still scrambling to finish their work.

"What was *that* all about?" Hal asked, once she was out of earshot.

I shook my head, wondering if maybe Heidi Bragg knew more about Amanda's disappearance than we did.

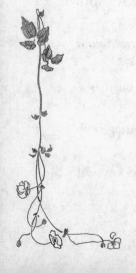

CHAPTER 5

The whole confrontation with Heidi made it nearly impossible to concentrate in French class. While Madame Booté (actual last name: Bouton, but renamed by students for obvious reasons) droned on about *le conditionnel passé*, I couldn't help thinking back to a conversation that Amanda and I once had about Heidi.

We were at Play It Again, Sam's, the thrift shop where we had discovered Amanda's box. Amanda said she needed a belt to go with her 1950s poodle skirt. But all she wanted to do was shop for me. And so she started pulling dresses, pants, and sweaters off the racks. Putting together outfits I'd never even dreamt of: a pencil skirt with a ruffled top; a long tube dress with a pair of knee-high boots.

Frilly scarves paired with basic T-shirts.

Leggings with a short jumper.

A fur vest over a sequined dress.

"I can hardly wait to see you in these clothes," Amanda said, setting me up in a dressing room.

"I take it you're not enamored of my style." I looked at myself in the full-length mirror. Wearing a black, boxy sweatshirt with a pair of sweatpants snatched from Cisco's dresser, I had to admit I wasn't exactly enamored of my style either.

"I'm enamored by all styles," she said, handing me a wide snakeskin belt. "The trick is to match the style with the occasion."

"And for what occasion does someone like me have to wear all this stuff?" I asked, glancing at the plethora of try-ons.

"Thrifting with a friend, for one." She laughed. "School for another, a day at the movies for a third . . . a stroll through the park, lunch by the pond, an afternoon at the museum—"

"I think I get it," I said.

"Good." She met my eyes in the mirror. "Because brilliance like yours is wonderful, but there are so many other layers to a star. Why just stop at the photosphere?"

"Well . . . ," I stammered, curious as to where she was going with all this.

"Not well, *and,*" she corrected me. "A star is also radiant, so let's work on getting you to express that radiance, too."

I waited for her to let out a laugh. But her expression remained serious. Apparently she meant it. I felt my face grow warm, glad when she finally shut the curtain so I could be alone to change.

It's just that aside from my mother—whose job by definition, among her many other parental obligations, is to boost my self-confidence as often as she can—no one had ever said anything like that to me before.

"Ready?" she asked after only a couple minutes.

"Not quite," I said, still struggling with a sleeve.

While Amanda saw style as something that helped illustrate her mood—a blond wig one day, a ballerina tutu the next—I saw it as something that detracted attention from what was on the inside.

"The problem with that theory," she said, once I'd tried to explain it to her, "is that by shrouding yourself, it's nearly impossible for anyone to get close enough to actually see the inside."

My jaw tensed, but I couldn't really argue. And so I maneuvered my way into my outfit: a formfitting sweater dress that came to the knee.

"Holy Hepburn," she said once I'd opened the curtain. "Audrey Hepburn, that is. You do realize how much you resemble her, right?"

"You don't think it's too purple?" I asked.

"Are you kidding? It's actually more plum than purple, plus it makes your brown eyes pop. Coco Chanel said, 'The best color in the whole world is the one that looks good on you.'"

She removed my clunky brown glasses and took out my ponytail so that my hair fell down around my shoulders.

"Audrey had a pair of chic cat-eye glasses that I think might be really striking on you."

"Really?" I asked, almost wanting to believe it.

"Well, what do you think?" She spun me around so I could look in the dressing room mirror.

I couldn't help but admit that I actually liked the way I looked, nor could I help the tiny smile that inched across my lips, even if it was a tad blurry without my glasses.

"'The nature of this flower is to bloom,' right?" she continued.

"Alice Walker," I said, giving credit to her quote.

While Amanda continued to shop around, I tried on the rest of the clothes and even ventured to pick out a few things on my own, ending up with a whole pile for purchase.

"Will your parents be okay with all this?" she asked.

"Are you kidding?" I said, gesturing to Cisco's sweatpants. "My mother will be thrilled."

I handed Louise my credit card. My mother had given it to me for just this purpose, though I had never used it before.

"Just remember that fashion is your friend," Amanda said, pulling on a newsboy cap.

"Your very best friend," Louise chimed in, handing me my receipt.

"It has nothing to do with impressing other people, or showing everybody how much money you have," Amanda continued. "So don't be afraid of it, or take it too seriously. Just enjoy it."

"Well, thanks," I said, wanting to tell her more—how

much the whole shopping expedition meant to me. "I feel really . . . it's just that this really means . . ."

"You're welcome," Amanda said, paying for her newsboy cap with a ten-dollar bill, and still getting change back. She wrapped her arm around my shoulder, as if she knew just what I was trying to say. "You're going to be simply smashing in these new clothes of yours. Just wait until Heidi sees you in that color-block dress. I mean, hello, Jackie O. No greener is the eye of envy."

"As if I'd even care," I said, surprised that she would bring up Heidi. "Plus, I doubt she'll even notice."

"Make no mistake," Amanda said with a squeeze. "Heidi notices everything. Don't underestimate her for a single second."

"Meaning?"

She stopped on the sidewalk and let her arm drop from my shoulder. "Just promise me you'll be wary of her, okay?"

Though I appreciated the warning about Heidi, it wasn't exactly necessary. Heidi and I had been major enemies since middle school. In retaliation for my turning her and her friends in for cheating, she'd concocted a scheme having to do with my crush: Keith Harmon. They created a fake email address for him, and used it to start writing me, making me believe that I was actually corresponding with him, and not them.

The whole thing was humiliating. I'd confessed to "Keith" how cute I always thought "he" was; that I'd love to go on a date with "him" sometime; and that, yes, I'd definitely sit with "him" at lunch. My friends at the time (those I subsequently ended up pushing away out of sheer mortification) had tried to warn me that this was all likely part of one big fat joke. But unfortunately I didn't listen. And so began my crash course in Stupidity 101.

"All I'm saying is to be careful who you trust," Amanda continued, avoiding my eyes, "especially when it comes to Heidi and her family."

"I get the message . . . Now, where are you taking me?" I asked as Amanda all but shoved me down the sidewalk and into another store: the eyeglass place, where we shopped around for new cat-eye frames.

"Nia?" Madame Booté asked, snagging me out of my reverie. *"Qu'est-ce que c'est le conditionnel passé du verbe donner, pour le pronom tu?"*

"Tu aurais donné." I yawned. Honestly, what was the point? We'd been reviewing *le conditionnel passé* for weeks. Why wasn't there an *advanced* Advanced Placement French course for people who actually study?

"Excellent!" she said, turning back to the board, where she'd listed a bunch of irregular verb stems.

I scanned the list, still stuck on Amanda's warning about trust. Because who was she to even talk about trust in light of all the lies she'd told us?

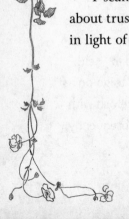

CHAPTER 6

At lunch, Callie, Hal, and I parked at what had become our usual spot in the cafeteria, close enough to the exit doors, but still far enough away from the kitchen so we wouldn't have to endure the scent of overly processed poultry.

"So, any ideas what we should say to that Waverly woman today?" I asked.

"Do you think it's crazy if we tell her we have the box?" Hal began. "And if we say we'll only give it to her if she answers all of our questions?"

"And what questions would those be?" Callie asked.

"First of all, we would *never* even consider giving that woman the box," I told them.

"Not even if we keep the *real* one and give her a fake one that we fill ourselves?" Hal suggested.

"Are you serious? Brittney has seen the box—tried to open it, remember? Maybe this Waverly did, too." Callie unraveled her tuna sandwich from its wax paper wrapping.

Hal shook his head. "No, it was a bad bluff. Too much TV. Sorry."

"We need to be careful about what we reveal to her," I said. "Because way too many people seem to be interested in our search—way too many of the *wrong* people, I should say. People with ulterior motives." I reminded them that even Thornhill, when he first hauled us into his office before he was attacked, kept grilling us about Amanda's whereabouts.

"Exactly," Hal said. "Why didn't he go to the police or call her parents right away?"

"Are you forgetting that her mother's dead, and her father's a dead-end mystery?" I asked.

"Not dead-end," Callie said, ever optimistic. "Just a mystery."

"How about her older sister?" Hal asked. "I mean, she's the one who supposedly has custody of Amanda."

"Try to even *find* Robin Beckendorf," I argued. "We have no idea who she is, or where she is. Not to mention that a Google search offered up nothing."

"Right, so maybe Thornhill had no other choice than to ask us," Callie said. "Maybe Amanda's files were all a bust, and he had no other leads."

I took a deep breath, knowing she had a point. Prior

to finding all that stuff in Amanda's box, none of us had been quite sure what the true story was with Amanda's family. Because we'd all been told something different.

While Amanda had told Callie that she'd been living with her grandparents in Orion (because the UN had posted her father in Latin America and her mother was studying gorillas in Uganda), she'd told Hal that her father was deceased, and that she and her mother had been living in some new condos downtown. Meanwhile, the story I got was that her parents were going through an ugly divorce, and that she and her mother were staying in a local hotel until they found more permanent housing.

"Let's also not forget all the bizarre questions that Officer Marciano asked me about Thornhill's attack," Hal continued.

"Or that doctor's questions at the hospital when we tried to visit Thornhill," I said, remembering how some of those questions had sounded curiously similar to Officer Marciano's. "Plus, why was Heidi's behavior even weirder than usual earlier? Since when does she care enough about Amanda to inquire about our search? On one hand, yes, people *should* be asking questions. Someone is missing, after all. But I feel like they're asking the wrong questions."

"It's because they have the wrong motives," Hal said, untwisting the cap from his bottled water.

"Maybe we're looking at it all wrong," Callie suggested. "I mean, the goal is still the same . . . to find Amanda."

"The goal *should* be the same," I corrected her, "but I'm not convinced it is."

"Agreed," Hal said. "Amanda isn't sending us all of these clues for nothing. She obviously doesn't feel safe enough to come out."

"I just want to find her," Callie whispered, taking a halfhearted bite of her sandwich.

"We all do," I agreed, "but we have to be smart here. Amanda is counting on us."

"And we can't let her down." Hal nodded. "That's why, aside from calling that Waverly person, we should also check out the address we found for Dr. Joy's rehab facility."

I took a bite of my chicken salad wrap, wondering if that's where Thornhill was right now. Callie and Hal found the address in Mrs. Bragg's safe-room-turned-office. The address was printed on her prescription bottle.

"Wait, didn't your friend Frieda say that Joy's clinic had been shut down?" Callie asked.

That was true. A few days before, Hal had taken a train to Baltimore to meet Frieda, one of Amanda's old artist friends. According to Hal, Frieda was acting "cloak-and-dagger-ish," requesting that he meet her at an old abandoned train station, and ordering him not to tell anyone about the visit. Apparently Frieda had been in touch with Amanda, though she wouldn't elaborate one iota. Instead she warned him about the dangers of the three of us being together, and then told him that Dr. Joy had gone into hiding.

"His clinic in Baltimore has been dismantled," Hal said, correcting her. "But not the rehab facility in Orion. It's definitely worth checking out."

"I'm game," Callie said.

"Me too," I said, suddenly wondering why I hadn't yet talked to Louise at Play It Again, Sam's to see if she might have any information about Amanda's sister, Robin. "Where should we meet?" I asked.

Just then, Traci of the I-Girls appeared at our table.

"We need to talk," she demanded. "In private."

I looked back at the I-Girl table, shocked that the invisible force field that seemed to surround it hadn't zapped her back into place. Kelli sat by herself, picking all the evil, carb-infested croutons from her garden salad with a pair of pink chopsticks that matched her sweater.

Traci flicked back her jet-black hair, awaiting my response. I would rather not chat with her at all, considering our recent run-in at the drama cast party. She'd made the mistake of calling me a freak and saying that I wasn't welcome, even though I'd done costume design. Thanks to Cisco's iPhone, however, I was able to text an invitation to the two hundred residents of his address book, thus mass-crashing the I-Girls' formerly exclusive event.

"Talking to you might be difficult considering that I'm trying to digest food," I told her.

"Yeah, well, I won't take up a lot of your digestion time." She smiled at Hal.

"State your business. I'm not going anywhere," I told her.

Traci looked irritated. She glanced over her shoulder to make sure that nobody was listening in and then took a step closer. "Okay, well, I just wanted to say that it was pretty lame of me to treat you like that at the cast party. I seriously don't even know *what* got into me."

"*Seriously?*" I said, half-mocking. Still, I nearly choked on my mother's Waldorf chicken salad at the sheer idea that Traci would even *attempt* an apology.

"Yeah, I mean, you had every right to be there. It was stupid of me to say that the party was just for the cast. I mean, just because it's called a *cast party* and doesn't include the word *crew* . . . I guess I get a little carried away sometimes. So, no hard fees, okay?" She faux-pouted.

"'Hard fees'?" I asked her.

"Um, *hard feelings,*" she explained with a roll of her eyes, obviously frustrated that I wasn't fluent in I-Girl.

I felt my forehead furrow, wondering if this was a joke, if at any moment someone might pop out of the soda machine and tell me I was on some hidden-camera reality show.

Traci didn't flinch for a second.

"I accept your apology," I said, considering the possibility of an insider I-Girl, one who might—and I knew it would be a long shot—be able to get us information from beyond the manicured walls. "No 'hard fees.'"

"Are you sure?" She smiled again at Hal. "Because I totally wouldn't feel right if you were still offended or anything."

Before I could answer, Heidi stormed up and inserted herself into our conversation. "Don't tell me you're joining the loser table, too." She glared at Callie.

Traci pressed her eyes shut, revealing a thick layer of sparkling bronze eye shadow that coordinated with her ballet shoes, as if her worst nightmare had just come true.

"Can you please tell me *what* exactly you're doing over here?" Heidi asked her, wielding her mighty force field. "Because it really isn't socially safe to venture over here."

"It was really no big," Traci said.

"If you're hanging out with dweebs, then it *is* a big," Heidi insisted, checking her iPhone to make sure nobody more important had tried to reach her.

"How about you leave her alone, Heidi," Hal said.

"Excuuuuse me?" she drawled, widening her eyes. "I'm surprised that you can stomach sitting here. If I were you, Hal Pal, I'd do myself a favor and break free of these dead weights. With a little work you might have a real shot at making the transformation."

"Transformation?" he asked.

"You know." She shrugged. "From dork to dreamy, from dweeb to steamy . . ."

Hal's gray-blue eyes narrowed at her. "You're the only dead weight here."

Heidi's mouth tightened, but she only said, "Nice, Hal. Just trying to help." At the same moment, her phone slipped from her grip. She tried to catch it, but it bounced off the table and landed in my lap.

"Hand it over," she hissed.

But for some reason, I wanted to hold it. I stared down at her pink screen, suddenly able to picture a series of text messages.

"*Now!*" she demanded.

I ignored her and closed my eyes. In my mind's eye I could see the texts flying furiously between her and Kelli.

"You little freak," she snapped. "Hand it over, or you'll be wearing chocolate milk on those secondhand clothes of yours . . . not that anyone would notice a difference."

"Oh, really?" I ventured, looking at her again. "Well, since we're on the topic, why don't you tell Traci what you and Kelli were texting about *her* clothes?"

"I have no idea what you're talking about." Heidi's overly glossed lips bunched up in confusion.

"You know . . . how she wears too much brown . . . how she's starting to look like a pile of crap."

Heidi snatched her phone back, nearly taking my hand along with it. But she didn't deny it.

"A pile of crap?" Traci gazed down at her outfit du jour: a brown suede minidress with chocolate-brown tights and bronze ballet slippers—just a couple shades off from brown.

"And that's not the only thing Heidi's texted about you," I bluffed, suddenly wishing I could take her phone back. "Do you want to hear what she had to say about Kelli? And about Lexi? About all your other friends?" I looked around, noticing how we'd attracted the attention of at least a dozen tables. Even Keith Harmon stared back in my direction, seemingly eager to hear more.

"Looking for your boyfriend to save you?" Heidi mocked, following my gaze. "Do I seriously need to remind you that Keith said he'd rather date farm animals than you?"

"Knock it off," Hal told her.

"Whatever," she said, waving the comment away. "Nia's lying. She has no idea what she's even talking about."

"Try me," I said, praying that she wouldn't call me on it.

Instead she backhanded my entire lunch at me. Chicken salad and chocolate milk landed in a messy heap all over my lap and the floor. "You're such a freak!" she shouted, soliciting even more attention. Her body was shaking with anger.

Hal stood up to block her from me. "What's with you,

Heidi?" he asked her, keeping his voice low.

Seconds later, Mrs. Watson came flying over and gave us all detention.

"But it wasn't Nia's fault," Callie said while helping me wipe off.

"It wasn't any of our faults," Hal added. He gestured to the four of us, including Traci.

We tried to plead our case, but Mrs. Watson wasn't hearing any of it. "You'll all have an opportunity to explain yourselves after school."

"But we're busy after school," Callie started to object.

"I guess you should have thought about that *before* you decided to start a food fight."

I shook my head, baffled by the whole thing—especially by how I was suddenly able to picture those text messages. Had they been part of a dream? Or something I had put together from a prior eavesdropping session? Was that even remotely possible? I racked my brain, searching for a reason that might make sense. But the only certain thing was that in all the years that I'd known Heidi—too many—I'd never seen her get that enraged.

Mrs. Watson looked on until we all cleaned up the mess—including Heidi and Traci, who grumbled the entire time about the toll this was taking on their manicures.

Meanwhile, Callie was completely distraught, not just because there was chicken salad on the front of her dress, too, but because she'd just realized that she'd forgotten to bring her sweats for gym class. "And you just know Coach Richards is going to give me a big fat detention for it," she said. "Which means a double detention."

"Which means you'll never get out of here today," Hal added.

"And we'll never get anything accomplished," I sighed.

Heidi and Traci went off to the bathroom to disinfect their cuticles, and Hal, Callie, and I stood by the exit doors, waiting for the period to end.

"I really wanted to get going right after school," I told them. "I don't have a lot of time as it is." My mother was on a constant need-to-know status about my where-abouts and ETA, especially since Thornhill was attacked, and I'd already lied and said that I had a Model UN meeting this afternoon. "My mother is expecting me to be home by five thirty."

"Well, I have to be done before then, too," Hal said. "I need to get to the music store before it closes."

"Can't you go tomorrow?" Callie asked him.

"Can't *you* borrow gym clothes from Nia?" he suggested.

"If only I *had* an extra set of clothes with me." I gestured to my milk-stained skirt.

"Well, isn't there anybody else you can borrow from?" Hal insisted.

Callie peeked over at Kelli and Lexi, engrossed in

what appeared to be a *major* conversation at the I-Girl table, but then shook her head.

"I suppose you can borrow mine." Hal sighed.

"Your gym pants?" She giggled. "They'll never fit."

"That's what alterations are for." He pulled a rubber band from around his wrist, but Callie looked less than convinced, gazing at his lanky body and then staring straight at his chest.

I couldn't help taking a peek myself, noticing how his pectoral muscles stretched the fabric of his shirt just so, and remembering a rumor I'd heard—that somewhere on his body was a tattoo. I'd overheard much speculation as to what it was and where it could be. Ideas ranged from a fire-breathing dragon on his back to a lightning bolt on his hip, and some barbed wire around his bicep. But somehow those images didn't seem fitting, considering that his current T-shirt had a dancing Twinkie on it.

"I don't know," Callie said. "Maybe we should just postpone our plans until tomorrow."

"Tomorrow might be too late," I said, glancing up at the cafeteria clock. There were only four minutes remaining until the bell rang.

Hal swung his backpack over his shoulder, readying himself to leave. "I think we should try to do both today—call that Waverly person and then look for the rehab place. What's the penalty for ditching detention?"

"*Two* detentions in Callie's case," I said to correct him.

"Okay, fine," she sighed. "I'll wear Hal's pants."

"But that still doesn't get us out of detention for Mrs. Watson," I pointed out.

"Leave that one to me," Callie said, waving off an explanation. She turned on her heel and headed out the door, just as the bell rang.

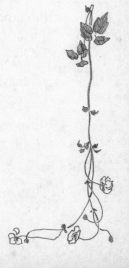

CHAPTER 7

Hal and I met in Mrs. Watson's classroom after school, fully prepared—and utterly disgruntled—to accept Watson's infamous sentencing of washing all the desks, crusty undersides included.

"Where *is* everybody?" I asked, wondering if maybe there was something we hadn't heard about.

I peeked out into the hallway just as Callie rounded the corner by the computer lab, hurrying in our direction. "I have some good news!" she shouted.

"*What*?" I asked, more than eager for a slice of this goodness.

"We don't have detention for Watson." Standing just in front of us now, Callie took a moment to catch her breath. "I got us out of it."

"How?" Hal asked.

Callie had indeed made magic happen. Not only did she wear Hal's sweatpants for gym, securing the extra slack in the waist and legs with rubber bands, and thus safeguarding herself from a double detention, but she also miraculously got us removed from Mrs. Watson's desk duty.

"I just promised her I'd compete in this math tournament thing she's been bugging me about." Callie shrugged as if it were no big deal, though I suspected otherwise. There was a reason why a genius like Callie had never taken Watson up on any of her sugarcoated offerings to compete in the past.

"The Math League?" I asked, trying to picture outgoing, exuberant Callie joining forces with a bunch of calculator-carrying mathletes. "I must say, I'm impressed." Not only was Callie coming farther out of her shell, but she was finally embracing her own natural intelligence.

"Definitely impressed," Hal said, flashing her a little smile. "And thanks."

"You're welcome." She smiled back.

"So, I believe we have a phone call to make," I said, ready to tackle this part of the mystery.

Hal nodded and I pulled out my cell phone.

"Wait, one question." I stopped in the corridor. "What about Traci and Heidi?"

"Oh, right," she said, trying to hold back a grin. "Well . . .

the offer only extended so far . . ."

Hal laughed. "In other words, they will be scrubbing desks by their lonesomes."

Callie sighed. "Sadly, yes." Collateral damage.

We moved to the area behind the football stadium, where there wasn't a lot of foot traffic. We sat on the ground, in the direct sunlight, and I set my cell to speakerphone so that Callie and Hal could listen in.

"Don't forget to block the number," Hal said.

I nodded, pressed star-six-seven, and then I dialed the number.

"Tea department?" a woman's voice answered.

I gave Callie and Hal a confused look, wondering if I'd gotten the number wrong. I rechecked the card.

"Is anyone there?" the woman asked; her voice was raspy and deep.

"Hi, is this Waverly Valentino?" I finally spoke.

There was silence on the line for several seconds, but then: "Who can I say is calling?" she asked.

My mouth hung open. No words came out.

"You'd like some tea, wouldn't you?" the woman asked, filling in the blank. "The medicinal blend is very popular this season. It contains elderflower and echinacea, which are good for flu symptoms, as well as the common cold."

"I'm looking for Waverly Valentino, please."

"I'm sure you'll like this blend," she continued, as if she didn't hear me. "It helps support the immune system."

"*Waverly?*" I asked, trying to determine if it was the same voice as the woman who had spoken with Cisco at the front door of our house.

"I'm glad you finally called. Your nerves must be acting up. We have a nice rose tea that would be soothing for that."

"But I have nothing to offer you in return," I said, referring to Amanda's box.

"Don't be foolish. Let's just meet to discuss your needs. Then we can come up with a solution for those pesky sinuses—I sense you are feeling pressure, or possibly some pain? I have a feeling you want to know *all* about the sinuses, am I correct?"

I shook my head, desperate to read between her confusing lines, decipher this code, and to know if she'd be any help at all with our search. "Does anyone by the name of Ariel work there?" I ventured.

"You certainly like the pricklier blends, don't you?" she said. "Just be careful. Those spicier types are apt to cause you some trouble."

"What kind of trouble?"

"Let this be a warning to you, Ms. Rivera: Don't go bothering your system with all those stinging nettles."

My body recoiled, just hearing my name. I knew I hadn't said my name. Plus I'd blocked my number.

"Where are you located?" I asked, eager to keep her on the line so I could think.

"Sunflower Street."

I exchanged more bewildered looks with Callie and Hal. For as long as I'd lived in Orion, I'd never heard of a street called Sunflower.

"I'm sure you'll be able to find it. Just be sure to bring along a nice sturdy box to carry all your teas. I hope to see you soon, Ms. Rivera."

"Don't hang up," I told her. "What number on Sunflower Street? Is that in Orion?"

But the line went dead. I waited a few moments to see if she would click back on. When she didn't, I snapped my phone shut.

"Well, that was obviously Waverly," Hal said.

"And she obviously wants the box," Callie said. "I mean, 'be sure to bring a nice sturdy box to carry all your teas . . .'"

"Seems like she's willing to give us information in exchange for the box," I said, referring to what she said about "telling" me about sinuses. "Not that that's even an option."

"Why do you think she was talking in code?" Hal asked. "I mean, did she have someone right there? Did she think her phone was bugged, or yours, for that matter?"

"Clearly, I have no idea," I said. "And if it were hard to talk, why give me that number in the first place?"

"Right," Callie said. "Why not a private cell line?

Why the number for a business?"

"And how do you think she knew it was you?" Hal asked.

"Who else *would* it be?" Callie said. "The woman gave Cisco her card. She was clearly expecting Nia to use it. And her name probably isn't Waverly Valentino. Let's take a wild guess that it's an alias she gave Cisco. Plus, how many young people do you think she has calling a place that sells tea?"

"If it's a tea *department*, then I wonder what kind of store it is, and what other departments they have," he pondered.

"Maybe Tea Department is the name of the shop," Callie offered. "I mean, I know it isn't exactly clever, but—"

"Then why not advertise the name on the card? And why an eye for a logo instead of a teacup?" I gazed out toward the soccer fields, where Cisco and some of the other players had emerged for practice. "Do you really think she expects us to show up?"

"Show up *where*?" Hal asked. "Because there's no Sunflower Street in Orion. Or when?"

I shook my head, because none of it made sense. Why would she tell me to come to a tea shop that didn't have a real name . . . on a street that didn't exist?

"I'll do some research," Hal said. "I'll check out all the street names within a twenty-mile radius. I'll also check out the names of herbal tea shops in the area."

"As well as homeopathic places," Callie added. "She

did talk a lot about treatment . . . like an herbalist or something."

"You know what *I* think?" Hal said, an irresistible grin curled up his face. "Amanda was smart to have us all work together." He extended his palm facedown in the air. "It's just like Heidi said; we're like the Three Musketeers, right?"

"Right," Callie chirped, placing her hand down over his.

I let out a sigh at how corny this was. But maybe, all things considered, a little bit of corny was a lot of what I needed. "Right," I said finally, setting my hand on top, and feeling a huge rush of heat charge over my skin.

CHAPTER 8

I'd written the address for Dr. Joy's rehab facility on the inside cover of my biology notebook. The facility was supposedly on the other side of town, but Hal was familiar with the area, having once taken a summer art class at Greyscale Charter School over there. We rode our bikes down winding streets, across a major bridge, and through at least four busy intersections before finally arriving at the place.

Only it didn't look like a rehab place at all. It was a small brownstone building with no signs outside indicating what it was. But on closer inspection through a picture window, it appeared to be a travel agency.

"What are the odds that someone would have had the time to dismantle an entire health care establishment and put another, completely unrelated business in its place in only a couple of days?" I asked.

"From the looks of it," Callie said, indicating the ads for cruises and flight deals that lined the walls, "I'd say pretty good."

"This is definitely the place." Hal pointed out the plaque by the door with the address clearly marked.

"So, why isn't there a sign?" Callie asked.

I shook my head. Phones were ringing; faxes were rolling in; brochures were being stuffed into envelopes and passed around the office. I looked back at the address inside my notebook, wondering if maybe I'd gotten it wrong.

But I knew that I hadn't.

"This doesn't make any sense," I whispered.

"What *does*?" Hal asked, perhaps feeling a bit defeated. "Are you forgetting your most recent phone call, along with everything else we've learned?"

"Plus, who knows?" Callie said. "Maybe this isn't a travel agency at all. Maybe it's just supposed to look like one."

"Well, if that's the case, then someone's doing a convincing job." I was parking my bike when I noticed something carved into the concrete.

A serpent with its body wrapped around a bowl. A black onyx had been set into the serpent's eye.

My hand clasped over my mouth, I remembered an

afternoon shortly before Amanda had gone missing, when she'd asked me to go for a walk through Orion.

"I realize you've lived here longer than I have," Amanda said, pointing us down Main Street. "But tell me, when was the last time you really looked at the buildings in town—really appreciated them for their architecture?"

"Hmm . . ." I paused for dramatic effect. "That would be never." The truth was that while I loved art and all things architectural, I never truly had appreciated those things in a small town like Orion. I suppose you could reasonably say that I ignored the beauty of my own backyard.

"Exactly." She laughed. "'To see what is in front of one's nose needs a constant struggle.'"

"George Orwell," I said, recognizing the quote.

"How much do I just love that you love literature almost as much as I do?"

"I'm guessing a lot." I smiled, happy to simply spend time with her—be it in Orion or anywhere else.

It was overcast that day, and Amanda was wrapped in a long pink trench coat with matching rubber boots. Her hair, as well (au naturel for a change, a pretty shade of almond-brown), was slicked back into a runway-model bun.

She pointed toward the doorway of the old town hall. "The detail is amazing. I keep drawing it in the margins of my notes in school." She readjusted her non-prescription square black glasses. "I love the archways and columns."

We continued up and down streets for several blocks, scoping out ornate window ledges and ivy-covered brick. It was thrilling to see the town like this—through Amanda's enthusiastic eyes—when all along I'd naively assumed that culture was reserved for places like Paris, Athens, and Rome.

"Are you interested in pursuing architecture?" I asked her. "In college, I mean?"

"I'm interested in pursuing everything," she said, pointing out a snakelike figure carved above the door of the bank. "Have you ever counted up all the bowl-and-serpent markings on the buildings around town?"

"Excuse me?" I asked, mentally preparing myself to be stumped.

"Don't even tell me you've never stopped to admire all the bowl-and-serpent markings?"

The truth was that I hadn't.

"You do know that there used to be a pharmaceutical college in town, right? Orion College of Pharmaceuticals . . ."

"I think I may have heard that," I told her. "The community center is one, I know. Isn't that where it used to be?"

"*Précisément.*" Amanda nodded. She informed me that many of the buildings around town—those with the bowl-and-serpent markings—were once owned by the college and used for various administrative offices and student housing.

"And now they're being used for places like banks and bakeries," I said.

"But things aren't always as they appear."

"Meaning?"

"Meaning there's more to the markings than meets the eye."

I looked back at the serpent above the bank door, noticing how its body was enveloping a chalice-like bowl. I knew I'd spotted some of these markings before, but being in a town I believed to be as culturally devoid as Orion, I'd never given them too much thought. "So what am I missing?" I asked.

"What about the symbolism? Ever heard of the Bowl of Hygieia?"

"From Greek mythology?"

"Exactly. Hygieia was the daughter of Asklepios, the god of medicine and healing. Hygieia's symbol was a bowl full of healing potion—"

"Which is why she's referred to as the goddess of health."

"I take it you're a devotee of Greek mythology, too?"

I nodded. "Ever since the third grade, when we learned about Zeus."

"Who was the grandfather of Asklepios," she added. "Anyway, the bowl and the serpent are seen together as a symbol for healing, which makes perfect sense for a town that once housed a pharmaceutical college, right? That's what I thought, too. But then I started really looking at the symbols themselves—studying them beyond simple college branding."

"And?" I asked, intrigued.

She turned to face me; her gray-green eyes widened. "There's something you have to know. Symbols and codes aren't at all accidental. Everything has a purpose."

"To confuse me?" I asked, completely at a loss.

"I think you'll understand better if I show you something." She led me down two blocks and around the corner. We stood in front of another building with yet another serpent-and-bowl marking. "Notice anything different about this one?" she asked.

I wanted to tell her I did. But I didn't. It looked exactly the same.

"Look closer," she insisted, taking me by the arm and bringing me up the front steps.

The serpent-and-bowl marking was about four feet tall and ran beside the double set of doors. But I honestly didn't see anything distinctive about it. I gazed up at the building's four stories of windows, the ivy that sprawled across the brick, and the old-fashioned fire escape with its iron balcony and staircase. "Is this an apartment building?"

"Could be."

"Well, there's no sign . . . there's nothing indicating that this is a business."

"But things are not always as they appear, are they?" she reminded me, pointing out the serpent's eye.

It was a black onyx.

"None of the other markings have this," Amanda explained.

"And this means . . . ?"

"So, there's something going on in there—something

that we need to check out."

"Because of an onyx eye?"

"I've been following the eye," she said. "Around town."

"It moves around?"

"Exactly," Amanda said, as if it all made sense. "When I was counting up all the marked buildings—twenty-three, in case you were curious—I noticed that the serpent marking on Jersey Street, the place with the red door, had the onyx eye."

"The shoe repair place?"

"Except it wasn't a shoe repair place at the time. It looked more like this one: a building with no signs. But still the onyx eye was there. It wasn't until after the onyx eye had been removed that the shoe place moved in. The same thing happened with a comic book store on Zephyr Street. When the eye was there, it was just a blank building. But just a few weeks later, the eye was gone and all of a sudden it was a comic shop."

"That's peculiar."

"More than peculiar. My bet is that something's going on inside these buildings," she said. "Something probably underground and corrupt. Someone is using the onyx eye as a marker for other people to locate them. And people must be closing in, too—people they don't want to attract, that is—because why else would they keep moving around?"

"Yes, but what is going on inside?" I asked.

"Good question." She smiled. "Care to find out if there's more than meets the eye?" She nodded to the entrance.

Part of me wondered if she was perhaps overthinking this whole serpent-and-bowl-onyx-eye business, but I was definitely captivated by the mystery. "Are you sure about this?" I asked.

Amanda didn't answer. Instead she slipped on an extra-large pair of sunglasses, despite the drizzly weather, and put up the hood on her raincoat, concealing her hair.

She tried to open the front door, but it was locked. Not surprising. If this were indeed an apartment building, one would need a key. I was just about to turn away when Amanda touched my shoulder to stop me.

The door had opened a crack.

A woman wearing a long white lab coat, with her hair held neatly in a net, looked us over carefully before opening the door wider so that we could go in. "Good afternoon," she said in a silky-smooth voice.

I took a step closer, noticing some writing over the breast pocket of her coat. The words ORION COLLEGE OF PHARMACEUTI-CALS were stitched there in black capital letters.

"Can I help you find something?" she asked.

A wide smile sprawled across Amanda's face, undoubtedly because her suspicions had proved correct. "If we could just browse around for a little bit?" she asked.

The woman nodded and went about her business. Meanwhile, we began ours.

The place had the look of an old apothecary—wooden shelves, old glass bottles, metal stands. It seemed almost from another time except for the products on the shelves. There were aisles and aisles of pharmacy stuff—from bandages and painkillers to cough suppressants and chewing gum. Pharmacists were busy filling prescriptions behind a large counter area, while a customer was getting not only a swab of his saliva but also strands of his wiry gray hair analyzed.

"Are you okay?" Amanda whispered, probably noticing the shock on my face. I mean, who would have thought she'd be right? What was this place?

"Are you sure this is your first time in here?" I asked her.

"Absolutely."

"Why do you think there is no sign outside indicating that this is a functioning pharmacy?"

"Like I said, this place is probably a secret. People probably only know about it through word of mouth." She pointed to the woman mixing flowers in a bowl and adding what appeared to be the entire contents of a bottle of vanilla extract. "Maybe not everything in here is on the up-and-up. Or maybe it's a front for something else."

"And the reason they stay in Orion, housed in the bowl-and-serpent buildings once owned by the college . . ."

"A girl only knows what's in front of her nose," she said, as if this puzzle couldn't get trickier. "And that's often the stuff that she does not see."

"Clarity, please?" I asked her.

"Maybe whoever's spearheading this whole underground organization has some sort of affiliation with the college, or with the person who purchased the properties." Amanda smiled and picked a handful of honey sticks from a pretty blown-glass jar. "I'm just guessing, of course. Nothing's set in proverbial stone."

"Aside from the onyx eye," I said, stating the obvious.

"And even that can change," she clarified, remaining dead serious. "The eye can be removed. It can be relocated someplace else."

"I suppose," I said, more than eager to leave.

"Look," she said, facing me again. "There's a lot about this town that you don't know. A lot of scientists. A lot of people experimenting. And a lot of shady business."

"How do you know?"

"Just keep your eye on the eye," she said, ignoring the question.

At the same moment, a woman whipping up an egg concoction stopped mixing to look at me.

"Let's go," I said.

"Not yet." Amanda moved toward a sign that read TEA TREATMENTS.

While she insisted on staying a few minutes, I exited out the double doors and waited for her outside in the rain.

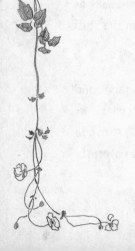

CHAPTER 9

"Are you okay?" Hal asked, pulling me out of my memories. We were still standing in front of the travel agency. I gazed back at the serpent-and-bowl marking, now realizing the connection: the eye on Waverly Valentino's business card matched the serpent's eye with the onyx stone.

"We should go inside now," Callie said, checking her watch. "Especially since you guys are so pressed for time. We can just pretend we're booking a trip and see what happens."

"Sounds good," I said, deciding to tell them about the serpent-and-bowl significance later, since we didn't have any time to waste. "But we really need to exercise caution in there."

"Okay, you're freaking me out a little more so than usual. Because . . . ?" Callie asked, sensing my unease.

"We're *always* careful," Hal said, before I could answer. "At least we always need to be where Amanda's involved."

"Fine. Let's go," I said, passing Hal my bike so he could lock it up with the others.

We entered the agency. A woman at the front desk hung up her phone. She was probably around twenty years old, with straight orange hair and layers of dark eye makeup. "Can I help you?" she asked, giving us the classic head-to-toe once-over.

"Yes, hello. We're interested in a trip," Hal ventured a little tentatively.

"I see," she said, still eyeing all three of us. "And where are you interested in going?"

We exchanged slightly hesitant looks, but then Callie took over: "Bermuda," she asserted, gesturing to a sign on the wall. "Daddy says I can have whatever I want for my birthday. And what I want more than anything else is for my friends and I to enjoy a relaxing time away from the everyday hell we call high school."

"I see," she repeated, seemingly unconvinced. "Does your daddy know that that's going to be a very extravagant birthday present?"

"Money's no object. Especially when it comes to me," Callie lied with aplomb. "Daddy likes to spoil me rotten."

Hal almost let out a laugh, but he was able to cover it up with a cough.

"Well, how about I give you some literature that you

can share with your daddy?" the woman said, still chilly.

"That would be great," Callie chirped, ignoring the agent's sarcastic tone.

While the woman fished inside her drawer for some brochures, I scanned quickly around the place. Despite the hustle and bustle of agents, we were the only customers inside—that is, until a familiar-looking man stomped in wearing a black baseball cap and dark clothing. I knew I'd seen him somewhere before. I recognized the slump of his posture and the lightning-bolt scar on his neck. The man went straight to an empty desk in the corner, opened up a folder he was carrying, and started sifting through the papers inside.

"Is everything okay?" one of the agents asked him.

"Just fine," he said, his voice rusty as nails.

And that's when it hit me—exactly where I'd seen him, and where I'd first heard that scratchy voice. The hospital when we went to visit Thornhill. I remembered seeing him talking to Thornhill's doctor—the same menacing doctor who asked us all those suspicious questions about our search for Amanda.

"Any deliveries?" he asked the agent.

The agent nodded toward a closed door at the back of the agency. The man responded by slamming his folder onto the desk. Seemingly preoccupied, he halfheartedly covered it with a couple of travel books. Meanwhile, my heart hammered inside my chest.

The man headed toward the closed office door, pausing

only once to glance back at the folder. He knocked twice, and then three quick times. The office door edged open, enabling him to scoot inside before it shut behind him.

My opportunity to check things out.

I went over to the corner desk, feigning interest in some brochures for Caribbean cruises, while Callie continued to query the woman about our fake trip. The man's folder was in plain sight, sticking out from beneath a copy of *Lady Liberty's Cheap Eats*.

I looked over my shoulder to make sure that no one was watching. Only Hal was. He gave me a confused look, at a loss for my plan. I motioned to the desk.

Luckily, he got the picture. And turned to reinforce Callie's battery of new questions to the agent. I could hear him inquiring about vacation resorts in Maui.

My pulse racing, I peered toward the back of the agency. The office door was still firmly shut.

In one quick motion, I moved the book and flipped the folder cover open, still leaving everything on the desk.

The page on top appeared to be a plot plan of some sort. In the bottom corner were the words *Casteel Airstrip*, and beneath that was an address, located in Saint Claude, just a few towns away.

I picked up the page to see more detail. Running my palm over the plan, I could fully envision an airplane hangar in brilliant Technicolor—a giant steel building with two dark blue stripes that ran across the front and sides.

I glanced back up to check on the agency. Things were

still bustling. People were on their phones. Agents were still typing away on their computers.

No one had noticed me yet.

While Hal and Callie continued to distract our agent, I grabbed the entire folder and started rifling through it. There were charts, graphs, and coding of all sorts—none of which made any sense. I tried to stuff the entire folder into my bag, which was bursting with books and home-work as usual. The inch-thick folder would not fit, so I went to shove it inside my coat, when something fell from it, landing on the floor with a ding—though to my ears it sounded deafening.

My eyes snapped shut. I could feel my stomach twist. But luckily nobody was looking my way. Cradling the folder in my arms so no one could see, I sunk to the ground, pre-tending to have dropped something from my bag. I fumbled with the zipper, finally noticing what had fallen.

A necklace. With an antique key.

It was Amanda's necklace. I would know it any-where. I picked it up and ran my fingers over the teeth. A flurry of images sprinkled across my mind, all related to the key: on a ring amid twenty other odd antique keys; stuffed beneath a mattress; palmed by a woman with brittle hands but perfectly manicured fingernails; inserted into the lock of a Victorian-style armoire with brass fixtures.

And then I saw an accident. A white car and a trail of blood. The key was clenched in the victim's hand.

My head started spinning and I felt myself get dizzy. I dropped the necklace into the pocket of the folder and fumbled to pull myself up. My face was burning and the fluorescent lights overhead stung my eyes. I looked back toward Hal and Callie. Hal was staring straight at me; his lips parted as if he could tell how distraught I felt.

I stuffed the folder into my coat. At the same moment, Hal tapped Callie on her shoulder and whispered something into her ear. She must have told the agent that we had to go, because the next thing I knew, Callie was shaking the agent's hand and moving to leave, a wad of brochures clenched in her hand.

Without a word, they followed me out. Hal struggled with the combination on his bike lock. Meanwhile, I urged him to go faster, almost tempted to abandon our bikes and hightail it out of there on foot.

"What happened?" Callie asked, sensing my distress.

"You took that folder, didn't you?" Hal said.

"Hurry up," I insisted, my knees about to buckle from nerves.

Finally, Hal managed to get his lock open on the third try. But he was still struggling with the one connecting Callie's and my bikes. Callie leaned down and helped wrestle the U-lock off our tires, and *pop*—we were free to ride. I grabbed my bike, hopped right on, and took one last look through the agency window.

The man whose folder I'd taken had returned from the back office. And he looked every bit as desperate as

I felt. He tossed books and brochures from the corner desk, obviously looking for the folder. I placed my hand over its bulk in my coat, feeling my heart beat even faster than before.

With each second I watched, the man grew more frustrated. A couple of agents came over to help him. Finally he cleared the desktop entirely with one brush of his arm. He shook his head, perhaps second-guessing himself. But then he turned in our direction, spotting us by chance.

And saw me watching.

Our eyes locked. And in that moment he knew.

"Let's go!" I shouted.

Hal and Callie leapt onto their bikes, and we all started riding furiously away, just as the agency door swung open.

"Stop!" he called out. He ran, much faster than I'd anticipated, just inches from Callie's back wheel. He managed to grab it, but she was able to keep on pulling away, losing his grip in an instant.

Before I knew it, he'd jumped into a car at the end of the street. I heard the ignition turn over.

The muscles in my legs ached as we went uphill toward a park, where I figured we could lose him. I pedaled hard, seeing Callie fly ahead of me.

The car's tires peeled out on the pavement just behind us. Still sweating, I moved onto the sidewalk, focused on the park.

Seconds later, I heard his car come to a screeching halt.

"Hold up!" Hal shouted.

I turned and saw that the guy wasn't chasing us anymore. He was out of his car, scurrying around on the street, retrieving papers that were blowing all around. It took me a moment to realize the papers were from the folder, and that the folder was no longer in my coat.

I'd dropped it.

"Let's go," Callie said, taking the lead. She headed toward a bike trail by the park. Hal and I followed. None of us looked back during the entire ride home. Nor did we speak a word.

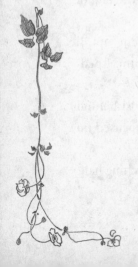

CHAPTER 10

We didn't stop until we reached the center of Orion—
only then could I catch my breath.

"I think we're good," Callie said, barely out of breath.

I looked over my shoulder, scanning for the man's
car, still feeling like we were being followed. For a second
I thought I'd spotted it—a dark sedan parked by the post
office—but when I blinked, I saw that the so-called car
was no more than a newspaper stand, and I knew that I
needed a break.

"So, what just happened?" Hal asked, his pale blue
eyes focused hard on me.

"That guy in the agency," I began. "Didn't you recognize him?"

"Not really," Callie said. "But then again, I was too

busy collecting travel brochures." She pulled a thick stack from her pocket.

"He was at the hospital the day we tried to see Mr. Thornhill," I explained, still rubbing my eyes after the newspaper stand hallucination.

"You recognized him?" Hal asked.

I nodded, frustrated that they didn't remember, but also aware that they probably hadn't even noticed him that day. I wouldn't have either, except my eyes had remained locked on Dr. Plummer as he'd scurried through a set of double doors with the security guard close at his heels. Dr. Plummer had been just a couple of steps away from an elevator when a man—the one from the travel agency—had stopped him, and they all glared back at us. That same man had been in the waiting area when we'd first arrived in the critical care unit. He'd been barking at the head nurse, but as soon as he'd spotted us he left out an emergency exit door.

"And you didn't think it was important enough to fill us in about Creepy Guy sooner?" Hal asked, once I'd filled them in.

"What, an arbitrary man with a scar?" I asked. "Pardon me, but between managing theamandaproject.com, investigating all these disparate clues, stealing top-secret folders, and breaking into the private offices of police chiefs' wives, this little detail slipped my mind. Plus, shall we even begin to rehash the list of things that you failed to tell *us* right away?"

"Yeah, well, moving on . . . ," he said, his proverbial tail stuck between his knees.

"It's just really weird," Callie said. "I mean, what do you think the guy at the travel agency was doing at the hospital in the first place? And why did you steal the folder?"

I proceeded to tell them about the folder, the charts and graphs inside, all with cryptic coding that I didn't understand. "If only I had been able to fit it into my bag . . ."

"Well, you tried. And the coding sounds similar to those lists I found on Thornhill's desktop," Hal said, referring to a file he'd discovered that disappeared before he could show it to us. When he clicked on it, he saw not only columns of data and rows of numbers but also a long list of people's names: our names, our parents' names, other students at school, as well as the names of people we didn't know.

"I also saw a plot plan for a place called Casteel Airstrip," I continued. "It's in Saint Claude."

"Saint Claude?" Hal said, surprise in his voice. "I think I might've seen a map of Saint Claude in Mrs. Bragg's office. At least, I'm pretty sure that was the name of the town. There was a giant X marked over an area."

"What area?" I asked.

Callie paused from fanning her face with a brochure. "Maybe Casteel Airstrip."

"We should definitely pursue that," I told them. Still suspicious that we were being followed, I gazed over both shoulders to check, but I didn't see anything that looked weird.

"Did you find anything else?" Hal asked.

I nodded. "The necklace."

"What necklace?" he asked.

"Amanda's . . . the key she used to wear . . ."

"Um, *what*?" Callie took a step back, completely unnerved. "Amanda never takes that necklace off."

"She'd never be without it," Hal agreed.

"I know. It was in that guy's folder," I said. "It dropped out, and I picked it up."

"Are you sure it was the same one?" Hal asked.

"Definitely sure. I touched it. I held it."

"*And?*" he persisted.

I swallowed hard. "And I had . . . well, what I can only really describe as a vision."

"A what?" Hal asked, his faced crinkled up.

"I know it sounds peculiar, but it was as if I could picture everywhere the key had been—on a key ring, inserted into a lock, being shoved beneath a mattress . . . and gripped in the hand of a car accident victim."

I knew that last bit would shock them, because we had recently gotten a newspaper clipping on theamanda-project.com about Annie Beckendorf, aka Amanda's mother, who was killed in a car accident. The article mentioned that when the officials discovered her body, Annie was clutching an antique silver key—just like the one Amanda always wore around her neck.

"Are you sure?" Callie whispered, clasping a hand over her mouth, her eyes tearing up.

I swallowed hard. "The same thing happened when I touched Heidi's iPhone—that's how I knew what she'd texted about Traci. It happened when I touched the *Ariel* book too: I could see everywhere it'd been—from an all-girls boarding school to the used bookshop where I think Amanda bought it."

"That's crazy," Callie whispered.

"I know."

"And we should definitely talk about it more," she said. "I mean, right?"

"Right. Sure. Let's talk. I just don't have any answers right now." I sighed.

"But first, why do you think that guy had Amanda's necklace?" Hal asked. "Or, more importantly, why does Amanda no longer have it?"

"He obviously knows something," I said. "He is somehow in league with someone. The question is, who? And why?"

"Even more reason to go check out that airstrip," Hal said.

"Are you both free after school tomorrow?" I asked.

"Count me in," Hal said. "I'll tell my parents I'm practicing with the band."

"I'm in, too," Callie agreed. "I have a sneaking suspicion

there might be an emergency mathlete meeting I have to attend."

"Great," I said, glancing up at the digital clock on the bank. It was 4:25. Hal still had enough time to make it to the music shop before it closed, and I had just enough of a window to stop by Play It Again, Sam's before dinner. With any luck, Louise would have some answers.

As soon as I left Callie and Hal, I realized that I'd failed to tell them about the serpent-and-bowl markings and the significance of the onyx eye. I'd have to call them both later.

I pedaled my bike feverishly, passing by the Villa en route to Play It Again, Sam's. Amanda and I had gone to the theater one Saturday afternoon for a screening of *The Wizard of Oz*. It was Amanda's idea to see it, and afterward we took a walk through Broadskill Park.

Amanda's face was aglow, and she was chatting on about how much she appreciated the Golden Age of Cinema and Victor Fleming's work as a director.

"You have to admit," she said, dipping into her bag of popcorn, "*The Wizard of Oz, Gone with the Wind, Dr. Jekyll and Mr. Hyde* . . . that man was a true genius."

"Well, I would not exactly argue. Victor Fleming, what can I say? Although, let the record show that I stand in awe of George Cukor, without whom the great screen goddesses could never have expressed themselves."

"Too true. Too true. So, then, tell me, what was your most favorite scene in this groundbreaking epic? In Kansas? In Oz?"

"I'm not really sure. On the ninety-seventh viewing, the scenes tend to blur together." I was joking, naturally. Judy Garland is, was, and will forever remain one of my very favorite entertainers. When I was twelve, I discovered the movie *A Star Is Born*. I'd liked it so much that my mother bought me the sound track. I'd lock myself in my room, grab a hairbrush for my mic, and pretend to be Esther Blodgett, singing about lost love.

"Ha! I'll get you, my pretty . . . ," Amanda said, calling my bluff.

"Okay, fine," I admitted. "It's not easy to choose, but I believe my favorite scene is when Tin Man, Lion, and Scarecrow go through the Haunted Forest, climb up to the witch's lair, and then manage to steal her broom for the great and powerful Oz, saving Dorothy from those evil monkeys."

"Because they were so brave, right?" she asked. "You like that scene because those characters exemplify bravery and heroism. They'd have done anything to help their friend, even if it cost them their lives. The Scarecrow, especially. He was torn to pieces and his arm got burned, but still . . . he does what he believes to be just. He actually does that throughout the movie . . . stands up for what he believes in."

"Are we still talking about flying houses, talking animals, witches, and broomsticks here?"

Instead of answering, Amanda stopped walking and turned abruptly to me. "You know you're the Scarecrow, right?"

"Not last I checked. I like to think I am dressing a lot more like Vivien Leigh in *Waterloo Bridge* now . . ."

"Okay, confession time." She sighed. "Because open and honest confession is abundant for the soul, right? Despite how much it pangs?"

"Wait, is that a proverb?"

"That instance in the library, when we were gawking at the Sylvia Plath book, that wasn't just a chance meeting. I'd planned it. I'd plotted it. Because I'd so desperately wanted to meet you."

"Excuse me?" I asked.

"About a week or so before we'd met at the library, I was in the school office. You were there, too. You didn't see me, standing at the back, but I heard you confront Thornhill, even after he'd threatened you with suspension for raising your voice."

I bit my lip, remembering the incident well. I'd been sent to Thornhill's office by Mr. Chinski, my English teacher, because I'd chosen to defend Peter Drake, a shy, reluctant student in the class.

Mr. Chinski clearly hated Peter, and he let him know it constantly, openly ridiculing his essays, mocking excerpts from his reading response journal, and calling on him more than anyone else, even though Peter rarely volunteered any answers. The final straw came when Chinski moved Peter's desk to the corner of the room, away from everyone else's, because Peter had been talking to Maria Katty. We were a little too old for the "time out" corner.

I honestly couldn't witness this behavior another moment, and so I stood up and told Chinski exactly what I thought: that he was a coward for having to resort to bullying those much younger and weaker than he was; that his abuse of power for his own egotistical benefit was appalling; and that he belonged in that corner, not Peter.

Jaws dropped. The room got quiet. Peter sat a little taller. And Mr. Chinski turned purple with anger. He ordered me to the office, where I told Thornhill exactly what I thought of my quote-unquote teacher and demanded that he do something about the situation himself, or else I'd take matters to the superintendent and the PTA.

"I knew that was great and powerful," Amanda continued, feeding the remainder of her popcorn to a family of ducks. "It was then that I knew I had to meet you—someone who'd stick up for what she believed in, whether or not it would benefit her in the end."

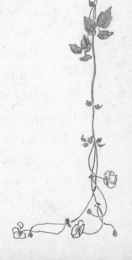

CHAPTER 11

A car on the street honked at me, disturbing my reminiscence, just as I rounded the corner by Play It Again, Sam's.

The shop had become my fashion oasis ever since my eye-opening trip there with Amanda. Usually fairly busy around this time of day—when people were getting out of work—the shop was surprisingly deserted when I entered. I even had to call Louise's name a couple of times before she finally appeared.

"Hey there," she said, emerging from behind a doorway of hanging glass beads. Her chocolate skin was glistening with a layer of peach-colored body glitter. "Like it?" she asked, referring to her most recent acquisition: a pair of creamy leather jeans, paired with a matching fuzzy sweater.

"Love it," I said, noticing how she glowed.

"I'm not sure yet if it'll stay on me, or go back on the rack, but sometimes I need to play dress-up, especially when the designer stuff comes in my size. So, are you here to play, too?"

"Not today," I said, taking a seat at the jewelry bar. "Today I just want to talk."

"Sounds serious." She slid a pile of flower-adorned headbands my way. Trying things on was her version of therapy.

My relationship with Louise had unexpectedly blossomed during my past several visits to her store. Another unexpected gift from Amanda. Even though it was obvious she had a secret side, Louise was the one adult I didn't feel so guarded around; she didn't expect me to be brilliant all the time. It was sort of ironic though. The first time I met Louise, I thought she was way too hard-boiled—thus not worth putting up with—for a conversation that lasted more than two minutes. But now, every time I saw her, it seemed like our conversations were never quite long enough.

"I'm glad you stopped by," she said. "It's such a refreshing change from all the, shall we say, 'interesting' characters I've had in and out of here the last couple days."

"*Interesting* characters?" I asked, checking out a headband adorned with a series of little stars.

"People buying handbags and then returning them a day later; and then quizzing me on what a girl your age would like . . . One woman didn't just want to know *what* I had for sale, but where it had come from in the first place, as if the Queen of England might've had it on her back . . ." Louise waved her hand in the air, as if whisking all that away. "Never mind my embittered prattling," she said. "What would *you* like to chat about? Fashion? Politics? Intriguing young men? Personally, I vote for the last, but I'm not just talking tragic heroes in literature and classic movie heartthrobs—not this time, anyway."

"I need to know about Robin," I said, with my usual tact and delicacy.

"Robin?"

"Amanda's sister," I explained.

"Amanda has a *sister*?" She raised her voice, feigning sincerity.

"You know that she does," I ventured, attempting to meet her big amber eyes.

But Louise looked away, fussing with the tag of her sweater. "This darn thing is making me so itchy. I'm thinking it is not mine to keep."

"Have you met her?" I asked.

Finally, Louise sat down next to me at the bar. She smelled like leather and lilacs. "Maybe once or twice."

"And you never thought to mention it?" I asked. "Do you know where she is? Because we obviously want to talk to her."

"Geez, Louise," she said, unable to get the sweater tag from digging into the back of her neck.

You may try to ignore me, I thought, *but I am known for my persistence.*

"Apparently Robin has custody of Amanda," I continued. "Amanda could be with her right now."

She stopped struggling and looked directly at me.

"I doubt it."

"Why?"

Instead of answering, Louise swiveled on her stool to grab a beret off a mannequin. "Here, try this on. I just got it in and I bet it'd look sharp with one of the shift dresses you bought last week. Long and lanky . . . that's the key." She winked.

"The *key?*" I asked, hung up on the word. I reluctantly pulled on the beret, hoping that she'd play nice as well.

Louise let out a long and audible sigh, clearly sensing my frustration. "Listen, I can only help you see the truth when you are ready to do so. Let's not force things before their time."

"Meaning I'm not ready now?"

"Look," she said, avoiding the question, and so I assumed the answer to be yes, "do you honestly think that if Robin had any answers about Amanda's whereabouts, she'd go blurting them to you?"

"What do you know?" I asked her.

She smiled softly at me. "I know that some rhinestone earrings would make that hat look even more smashing." She began to dig through a heap of jewelry.

"I have to go," I sighed, standing up from my stool.

"Nia, wait, don't leave. I'm not finished talking to you yet."

"But you're not saying anything."

"Listen here." She reached out to touch my forearm. "If Amanda is hiding out somewhere, don't you think she must have a darn good reason? Maybe it isn't safe for her to come out right now."

"I know."

"Well, then . . ."

"I just miss her," I said, hating myself for sounding vulnerable. "And I want to make sure she's okay."

"We all want that. And don't think twice about it: You may miss Amanda something awful, but she's with you . . . every day."

"I know." I rolled my eyes. "She watches us, she sends us clues, she plays with our minds regularly."

"That's not what I meant." Her face turned serious. "I mean, she's *with* you. She's become a part of who you are. You have to admit you're not the same girl who came through that door just a couple months ago. And I'm not just talking style, babe." She gave a nod to my snake-skin boots.

"I suppose," I said, somehow feeling reassured.

"Now do me a favor and try on those earrings."

I smiled, convinced that admitting to knowing Robin was about the extent to which Louise was willing to

go on the topic—for now at least. And so I held the earrings up and looked in the mirror, surprised by how
elegant they looked with the beret and awed by Louise's
insight, however oblique.

CHAPTER 12

My mother took one long look at me when I came through the door and peeled off my coat, her big brown eyes narrowing in disapproval. "What, may I ask, happened to you, young lady?" she inquired.

At first I thought it was the new beret and earrings (she sometimes has to adjust to my more unusual choices), but no, I had stashed those in my bag. Then I assumed I must still look harried because of the whole travel agency incident. But then she pointed to the giant chocolate milk stain on the front of my skirt.

"It was a rough day." I shrugged.

"What happened?" she repeated. Wearing stiletto heels and an apron-covered silk sheath, my mother was Betty Draper with a BlackBerry, couture wardrobe, and enough volunteer responsibilities to make most Fortune

500 businessmen weep with exhaustion. Or at least that's what my father says.

"A girl took issue with something I said at lunch."

"Why this time?" she asked, folding her arms, revealing her freshly manicured fingernails.

I shrugged again, and furrowed my brow. "Basically, she'd berated some classmates, and I confronted her about it."

"Do you really expect to make friends that way?"

"Would I want to be friends with a person who derides other people?"

My mother couldn't argue. Instead I spotted the tiniest of smiles inch across her lips, like maybe she was proud of me. "Go change and wash up, and then if you wouldn't mind giving me a hand sealing up the remainder of the auction invitations before dinner . . ."

Grand.

In my room, I peeked inside my closet to make sure no one had touched Amanda's box. Not that I'd expected it; it was just that one never knew how thorough—aka obsessive-compulsive—my mother could get on any given cleaning day. Apparently this auction was keeping her very preoccupied.

I changed into a formfitting black tunic and a pair of matching capri leggings, and then I plunked down at my vanity table. A smattering of makeup products stared up at me. I'd purchased them on a whim after one of my trips to Louise's shop.

Picturing Audrey Hepburn—since my outfit was a clear homage to her wardrobe in *Sabrina*—I spent a few minutes lining my eyes with a smoky charcoal color and adding mascara to my lashes. I contrasted the bold look of my eyes with a pale peach lipstick. And, for the finishing touch (since I was having some fun), I hiked my hair up into a high ponytail à la Audrey, and combed my bangs down so that they fell straight across my forehead.

"Nia?" my mother called from downstairs, eager for my envelope-licking skills.

Before heading downstairs, I peeked into Cisco's room, wondering why she wasn't beckoning for his help, too. Not that I should've been surprised: Cisco was famous for getting out of chores like this. And it appeared that he'd achieved said feat once again; there he was, lounging on his bed, reading a copy of *Soccer Nation*. He held a finger up to his lips. "Ssh," he whispered. "Thanks, Ni-Ni."

I gritted my teeth and refused to answer. He knew I hated that baby nickname.

Meanwhile, in the kitchen, Mama was elbow-deep in invites, while the tantalizing smell of her standard weeknight rice and beans filled the room. "I just want to finish up this last bunch," she said, her fingers working nimbly, stuffing auction invitations into their respective envelopes. "Would you mind helping me seal?"

"Sure. Where's Cisco, by the way?" I asked, stirring the pot and feigning ignorance.

"Homework. He has so much work to do, and he needs to keep up. Soccer has been taking up a lot of his time."

"Right," I snorted, grabbing an envelope. I stuck my tongue out to lick the cockroach-egg-laden glue (or so I've heard) when it suddenly occurred to me: "I think this will go a whole lot faster with a glue stick."

"Good idea. It really does pay to have a genius in the family," Mama said. "There's one in my office: top drawer on the left. And while you're at it, would you also mind grabbing the yellow sticky on my desk? It has a couple addresses of new parishioners that I want to include as well."

I nodded as I headed toward my parents' office. The dining room table was already set, and today's newspaper was already positioned on the living room coffee table, awaiting my father. I opened the door to the office and flicked on the overhead light.

Decorated in soft jewel tones with upholstered fabrics, the office is my parents' private space, which they insist on keeping a kid-free zone most of the time. I never really ventured in there but I was always impressed by how tranquil the room felt.

My mother's desk was as tidy as the rest of the house, making the glue sticks easy to find. Except I couldn't see the yellow sticky anywhere. Only a couple of manila folders sat on the surface of her desk, along with a tall ceramic vase and a family photo taken the summer before when we went to Niagara Falls. I grabbed the top folder, labeled *Church Auction*, figuring the sticky note must be inside. I started to sort through the folder's contents. It was full of brochures for possible venue sites, notes about caterers, and lists of donated items.

And then I came to another list.

A long list of names.

At first I assumed that it must be the list of volunteers or invitees, but then I saw the familiar names—my name, my parents' names, Callie's, her mother's, Hal's, his family's, and some people at school—and it suddenly dawned on me what this really was.

The same list that Hal had found on Thornhill's desktop.

My mind raced, but I tried to keep cool to avoid overlooking anything.

How were my parents involved?

I flipped the sheet over and saw the coding: the long rows of numbers and the columns of symbols—just like what I'd spotted in the folder at the travel agency. At the top, as a heading, it said C-33.

"Nia? *Pollita?*" Mama called. "Did you find that sticky?"

Her voice made me jump. I accidentally dropped the folder and its contents shot out everywhere. I scurried to retrieve them, accidentally bumping into the vase. It tumbled from the desk, but I managed to catch it in midair. As I snatched it, I spotted a folded envelope taped to the bottom.

"Just a second, Mama," I shouted back to her.

With trembling fingers, I pried the envelope off of the vase. Luckily, it hadn't been sealed. I opened it up, surprised to find a photo of a man, probably in his mid-twenties, posing for the photo with his fist propped under his chin. I looked closer, noticing how familiar he seemed.

Then it hit me: It was Thornhill, only younger.

Wrapped around his finger was what appeared to be a hospital bracelet fashioned into a ring—just like the one from Amanda's box.

"Forget the sticky, Nia," my mother called; her voice was getting closer. "We need to finish up before dinner."

My fingers shaking, I fumbled to stuff the photo back inside the envelope, and reaffix it to the bottom of the vase. But I needed more tape. I reached inside my mother's drawer, hearing her footsteps from only a room away. I tore myself a long piece, taped the envelope back in place, and then set the vase down on the corner of her desk.

My heart pounded as I hurried out of the office, coming face-to-face with my mother two steps beyond the door. "I couldn't find the sticky," I told her, trying my best to be completely composed, even though my pulse was absolutely racing.

"Did you find the glue stick?" she asked, looking at my empty hands. Her lips thinned in irritation.

"I did," I say, realizing I'd left it on her desk. "But

then I put it down again, I guess I was so busy looking for the sticky . . ."

"What's gotten into you? For goodness' sake, never mind. Go wash your hands for dinner," she ordered. "Everything's just about ready."

I nodded, eager to get away, even for just a few moments. Instead of heading to the bathroom to wash my hands, though, I hurried to my room to give Hal a call.

Luckily, he picked up right away: "What a coincidence," he said. "I was just going to call *you*."

"Why?" I asked instinctively. "Did something happen?"

"No." He laughed.

"Then you figured something out? Did something come in on the website?"

"Not exactly."

"Then what?" I asked, frustrated that he was not being clear.

"Well"—he cleared his throat—"I was just kind of wondering if maybe you weren't busy tonight."

"*Why?*" I said again, growing more agitated by the moment.

"I fixed my guitar strings and I need your honest opinion about the song I've been working on for the show. Any chance you can come over?"

"Are you serious?" How could he possibly think about music at a time like this?

"Look, if you're too busy . . ."

I bit my tongue, holding back from reminding him

that we had way more pertinent details to discuss than a song for the high school talent show. Instead I told him to call Callie and have her come over as well, figuring we'd still have an opportunity to talk. "We definitely need to get together tonight. I'll be there in an hour and a half," I said, hoping my parents would agree to it.

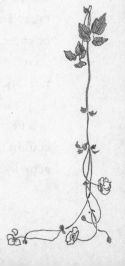

CHAPTER 13

Dinner at the Rivera household was normally around eight, but ever since my mother became the chairperson of the auction committee, our once set-in-stone dinnertime had been crossed out and penciled in.

My nerves finally quieted down, and I joined my family in the dining room. Of course my father was home now, and he gave me a hug as I came around to my side of the table. Traditional as my dad is, he does try to show me that he cares. He sat at the head of the table, while my mother served her famous food: chicken tamales, red beans over rice, and her legendary pork-stuffed arepa bread.

I sat down opposite Cisco, who, despite being engaged in a heated discussion about soccer players with my father, couldn't stop eyeballing me, and I thought I might've actually seen him give me a thumbs-up.

"Nia, you look nice," my mother said, just noticing. She nodded for me to take the teepee-folded napkin off my plate and place it on my lap. "New outfit?" she asked, as if there had never been a conflict over the glue stick.

"Old-new. I got it at Louise's."

"Pretty." She smiled. "Your makeup looks pretty, too. That shade of eye shadow really brings out the gold in your eyes."

"Going out tonight?" Cisco asked.

"Is that okay, Mama?" I asked, as she passed me the bowl of rice. "I'm already a week ahead of my classmates on homework assignments, and I spent my free period today studying for my French quiz. Plus, maybe Cisco could drive me . . ." I gave him what I hoped was a cajoling smile.

"Where do you want to go?" she asked.

"Hal asked if I could help him prepare for the talent show."

"You've been spending quite a bit of time with this Hal boy, haven't you?" my dad weighed in.

"It's not like that," I said, able to read his suspicious mind. "Callie will be there also."

"You guys went out after school today, didn't you?" Cisco asked. "I thought I saw the three of you heading off campus."

"Not me," I lied, giving him the evil eye. Did he not know anything about the sibling rule; i.e., I-scratch-your-back-you-scratch-mine? "I had a Model UN meeting. I have another one tomorrow. We had to end things today right in the middle of a debate about child labor laws in India."

"Oh, right, sure, right," Cisco said. "My bad."

"Definitely bad," I muttered.

"Well, I'm glad you're making friends, and your father is, too," Mama said, giving him a firm look. "Hal seems like a nice boy. And Callie is a lovely girl. We enjoyed having her here for dinner. So sad about her mother. Just plan on being home by nine thirty. Cisco can pick you up."

"Sounds good," I said, feeling the sweat on my palms, grateful that they didn't object to me going out on a school night. But I knew that my mom at least liked the idea of my being social, taking more than five minutes with my face and hair, and not hiding beneath layers of dark sweatshirts.

Surprisingly, Cisco didn't argue about being my chauffeur for the evening. He was far too busy being lectured by my parents, both of whom wanted him to give Father Bellows a hand cleaning up the rectory yard.

About a half hour later, Cisco pulled up in front of Hal's house and put the car in park. "I'm assuming you're here to talk about Amanda," he said, turning toward me.

"Because someone like me could only have been invited here for my problem-solving skills?"

"That's not what I meant." He sighed.

"For your information, what I said at dinner was true: I'm here to listen to Hal's talent show routine. He wants my feedback, and I promised I'd give it."

"Oh, really?" He paused to study my face, most likely searching for a flinch or flutter—something to indicate that I wasn't giving him the full scoop. "And since when are you so interested in the talent show? Or anything else non-curricular, for that matter? I mean, can you honestly tell me that this visit to Hal's doesn't have some sort of mystery-solving agenda?"

I looked away, knowing that he had me pegged. For as long as I could remember, my life had been wrapped up in work—in studying hard, in doing what was right, in learning as much as I could. There wasn't really room for anything else.

"Look, I know you've been working hard on the Amanda Project," he continued. "But I don't want you to keep secrets from me. Tell me where you're going. I'll drive you. Just keep me in the loop. If not, Mama's gonna hear all about it."

"Playing hardball, are we?" I raised an eyebrow at him.

"It's called looking out for my sister's best interests."

"I know," I said, admittedly grateful for his concern, but still smarting that he knew me way too well.

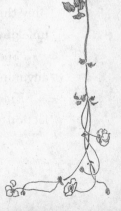

CHAPTER 14

Hal sat in the center of his room, his guitar music all set up in front of him. "Have a seat." He motioned to a stool, piled up with books.

"Is Callie coming?" I asked, surprised that she wasn't already here.

Hal nodded and started tuning his guitar—plucking at the strings, listening to the notes, and then tightening the pegs accordingly.

"When?" I asked, still bewildered that he could possibly think about the talent show in light of all that was unfolding.

"Soon," he answered. "She should actually be here any minute."

I moved his books and sat down, noticing his collection of Pez dispensers. At least two hundred of

them—from Wonder Woman Pez to Pez–Perez Hilton—
lined the top two shelves of a bookcase.

"Do you like Pez?" he asked, following my gaze.

I looked back at him, wondering if he was being serious. But his wide eyes and hopeful smile told me that he
was. And so I shrugged to be polite.

"So, what's the deal?" he asked, sensing my agitation.
"I mean, you obviously have something on your mind. Is it
something about Amanda?" I could see the disappointment
on his face—he thought I didn't want to hear him play.

"It can wait until Callie comes," I said, feeling a twinge
of guilt, and surprised to learn that, like Cisco, Hal had
me pegged, too. "What's the name of the song you'll be
performing?"

"'Believe in Me,'" he said, focused on his strings again.
"One of the band members wrote it."

"Okay. Let's hear it," I said, trying my best to sound
enthusiastic.

Hal spent a few more seconds plucking at the strings
before finally beginning the song. His voice sounded
sweet and earnest enough, but it was the music itself—
the combination of lyrics, chords, and rhythm—that sent
chills all over my skin.

"So, what do you think?" he asked after the last note.

I reluctantly opened my eyes, disappointed that the
song was over.

"I mean, it's still a little rough," he added, resting
his guitar on his lap.

"It was amazing," I said, hoping he believed me, because it was the truth.

"Seriously?" He perked up. "Because I've never really played solo for anyone before . . . anyone besides Amanda, that is. She used to like to lie in the grass, stare up at the sky, and listen to me play. Sometimes, she'd take out her notebook and draw or write for a while. I know it sounds kind of weird."

"It actually sounds completely *her.*"

Hal nodded and continued to thrum the strings. "Anyway, I really value your opinion. I know you never hold back, so I figured you'd be the perfect judge—jury and executioner if necessary." He laughed nervously.

"Well, thanks," I said, looking toward the wall, where there was an abstract portrait of a girl lying in a field of tall grass. I assumed that it was Amanda. "So, do you think I could hear some more?" I nodded to his guitar.

"For real?" He grinned, completely surprised.

I was surprised, too—surprised at the fact that, though I hadn't yet shared any of my news, Hal's music was calming me down.

Hal played "Angel Eyes" by Frank Sinatra. It was melodic and soulful, and reminded me of a trip my family and I took to Barcelona, where we had dinner at an outdoor café by the water, and a street musician entertained us with his guitar.

Hal's fingers were perfectly nimble as he plucked, pulled, and tapped at the strings like he'd been doing it forever. When the song was over, his eyes locked on mine as if maybe he had an agenda, too.

"What?" I asked, when he didn't say anything right away.

"Can I ask you something?"

"Sure." I nodded.

"All that stuff you've been talking about . . . about how images come to you when you touch certain objects . . . is that something new or has that always happened?"

I looked away, thinking back to a time in middle school when I was helping my dad find something in the attic. I came across Grandfather Rivera's old military hat. I touched it and a flood of images practically overwhelmed me. I pictured an old army barracks, a huge explosion, and a hospital unit with rows of injured soldiers. At the time I figured I'd just been remembering something I'd been told before, that somehow I must have known my grandfather's war history even though neither of my parents had ever spoken—or would speak—about it.

After that experience with the hat, nothing like that had happened to me since. Until I met Amanda.

"Pretty new, I suppose," I told him, reluctant to share the hat story.

Hal nodded, seemingly satisfied with the answer, but I could tell he wanted more. Before I could elaborate, however, there was a knock on his bedroom door. Mrs. Bennett edged the door open to reveal Callie just behind her.

"Hey," Hal said to her, practically beaming. The glow

of his face was like a megawatt bulb.

"Sorry if I'm late," Callie said. Her face was glowing, too.

She took a seat on Hal's beanbag chair. In doing so, a spray of beanbag filling shot out from somewhere behind her, landing in her hair. Callie let out a giggle, and Hal laughed along. His Ken-doll blue eyes made a zigzag line down the center of her face, landing on her raspberry-stained lips. And suddenly I felt like the third wheel on Barbie's Malibu beach bike.

"So, shall we get right down to it?" I asked, eager to break things up. "Because we definitely have some important issues to discuss."

"Like what?" Callie asked, leaning forward on the chair.

I told them about the list I found in my mother's auction folder.

"Just like the file I found," Hal said soberly.

"Exactly," I agreed. "Only the difference in this case was that the list in my mother's office had the header 'C-33,' whatever that means."

"I think Thornhill's file did, too, come to think of it, or at least that number was on there," Hal said.

"So, then, what does it mean?" Callie asked.

"Exactly. And why does my mother have a copy of it? A copy that's not exactly hidden away, but on her obsessive-compulsively neat desk, in the very folder that she's been working with."

"Meaning it's something she's looked at recently," Hal

said, articulating my actual concern.

I looked down at my lap, feeling the anxiety creep back into my stomach. "Is it possible that my parents are part of this whole mess?" I ventured, hearing my voice tremble over the words.

"Maybe," Callie said. "But you have to remember, our names are on that list, too. And it's not like we're conspirators, right?"

"And my parents? They are not really striking me as super-spies or anything," Hal added.

"Okay, so how do we explain the fact that I also found a snapshot of Thornhill wearing the hospital-bracelet-turned-ring that we found in Amanda's box?"

"In your parents' office?" Callie asked.

"Hidden under a vase," I clarified.

"Wait, *what*?" Hal asked.

"It's true." I nodded. "I practically knocked a vase over and found it hidden underneath. Very deliberately *taped* underneath, I might add. And why? I didn't even think my parents knew Thornhill."

"And you're definitely sure it was Thornhill in the photo?" he asked.

"Definitely."

"And you're absolutely positive that the ring around his finger was a hospital bracelet?" Callie asked. "Because it must've been pretty small in the photo . . ."

"Yes, but I could still make it out," I told her. "It was a close-up shot, so I was able to see Thornhill's face *and* the baby bracelet. I obviously couldn't make out any of the actual type, but it was clearly from a hospital."

"So then maybe it was someone else's hospital-bracelet-turned-ring," Hal said.

"Are you even listening to yourself?" I asked. "How many other hospital-bracelet-turned-rings have you come across in your lifetime? Bottom line, Thornhill's obviously even more connected to all this than we thought."

"Or at least he's connected to someone named Ariel Feckerol," Hal said, referring to the name on the baby bracelet in Amanda's box.

"And that Ariel person must also be connected to Amanda." Callie nodded. "I mean, why else would Amanda keep Ariel's bracelet in her all-important box?"

A second later, there was another knock on Hal's door. His younger sister, Cornelia, stood in the doorway with her laptop under her arm. "Did someone say Amanda?" she asked. Without even waiting for an answer, or for permission to come and join us, she took a seat on Hal's bed and flipped open the cover of her laptop. "We're way overdue for an update."

Cornelia was only in the sixth grade, but she acted more like one of the middle-aged detectives on *CSI*. An absolute guru of computer design, she was the one who created the Amanda Project website for us.

"Can't you see that we're a little busy talking here?" Hal asked her.

"And while *you're* busy talking, time is ticking, and

Amanda's still a no-show. So, are there any comments, details, or additional clues to share?" Her fingers rested firmly over her keyboard, ready to type as we dictated.

"Ignore him. Glad to see you. What additions have you made since the last time?" I sat next to her.

"Well." She angled the laptop so we could see the screen. "I've already put in a blurb about the first-edition copy of *Ariel*. Nia, I'll need to come over and take a photo of that—stat. And please"—she rolled her eyes—"tell me the lipstick heart hasn't totally been obliterated, though I know that at least part of it has, because otherwise I'll be forced to describe the original look and/or replicate it in some way, which, as you can probably guess, isn't the most authentic. I also added the information about the business card—*another pic needed, please.* And I posted a call-out to people for the 411 regarding herbal tea shops in the area, a street named Sunflower, and any news on Amanda's alleged aunt . . . a woman by the name of Waverly Valentino."

"Wow," I said, utterly impressed.

"I've been feeding her information as we get it," Hal explained.

"I also did my own online search for Sunflower Street," Cornelia said. "But I came up dry."

"And how about herbal tea shops?" Callie asked.

"There's one an hour away in Stoughton," she said, minimizing the Amanda Project screen and clicking on a spreadsheet entitled *Amanda Leads Too Preemie and/*

or Privileged to Post. "But I doubt that's the one. It was a different number than on the card and when I called them, they answered with the name of their shop—Tea-licious—rather than saying 'tea department.' I asked them if they even had an official tea department, which really confused them, and they were even *more* confused when I asked for an herbal tea remedy to help get rid of freckles." She pulled a strand of her dark red hair over her nose, perhaps trying to mask the spray of freckling there.

"Did you look up witch doctors, too?" I said, only partially joking.

"*I* started to," Hal said. "But there isn't exactly a listing labeled 'Wizards, Witches, and Sorcery' in the yellow pages."

"Practitioners of folk magic *do* exist," Cornelia corrected him. "But I'd suggest looking under something a bit more user-friendly . . . something like New Age Apothecaries, Naturopathic Medicine, or Herbal Remedies."

"Listen to you." Hal smirked at her.

"Whatever," she said, rolling her eyes for a second time. "Will that be all?"

"No." I shook my head. "There's actually one other thing we should add to the site." I spent the next couple minutes filling them in on my visit to the pharmacy with Amanda, and the whole bowl-and-serpent-with-the-onyx-eye mystery.

"See." Callie plopped down on the bed. "I knew that travel agency was a front for something else."

"But what?" Hal asked.

"I can't even believe that Amanda would notice something as tiny as a black stone in the eye socket of one of those serpents," Callie said. "I mean, those markings are all over town."

"Or at least they're on all the old Orion College of Pharmaceuticals buildings," I clarified.

"Still, I barely even give them a second look," she said.

"But I suppose we will *now*," Cornelia chimed in. "As will others, especially once we post a photo of the serpent-and-bowl on the site."

"So, that's obviously why Waverly Valentino's card has an eye," Callie said. "She's part of this somehow."

"And for all we know, that pharmacy you visited with Amanda," Hal began, focused on me, "was the same place we called when we phoned Waverly."

"Except that pharmacy was on Rantoul Street," I told them. "Not Sunflower."

"Maybe the pharmacy moved," Callie said. "Or else 'sunflower' is more code."

"Let's go check it out," Hal said. "At the very least to see if that onyx stone is still there."

Cornelia didn't look up for a second as she typed all the information in. "Give me twenty-four hours," she said, slamming her laptop cover shut. "I'll have it all up and live. In the meantime, get me pics—jpegs, preferably 300 dpi. Get me an address for some of these serpents. And be sure to email me with any more info." She pulled a stack of business cards from her pocket, and handed a bunch to each of us. "Feel free to pass these out to your friends and family members."

I knew better than to laugh as I read the card over:

GOT A MISSING FRIEND?
Get a Smarter One with Web Design Skills

CORNELIA BENNETT

Specializing in Web Design Services
to Help Get Your Loved Ones Found

Ask about our special first-time client rates

savvycb@yahoo.com

Cornelia would never forgive me.

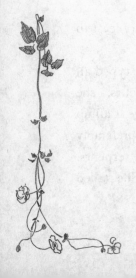

CHAPTER 15

As soon as Cornelia left, Hal was determined to go check out the pharmacy. *Tonight.*

"Why not?" he asked.

"Maybe because we all have something called a *cur-few*," I said.

"I'll tell my parents we need to go to the library for a project," he insisted. "I'll have my mom drop us off, and we can walk from there."

"I'm game," Callie said, her father being the most lenient of all our parents.

I glanced at the clock. It was just about 8:15. "Yes, but Cisco's picking me up in an hour."

"Couldn't you ask him to pick you up a little later?" Hal asked.

"I'll call my parents," I said, reaching for my phone,

wondering what I could possibly give as an excuse. But before I could even dial, there was yet another knock on Hal's bedroom door.

"Come in," Hal said.

The door edged open and a boy walked in. With shaggy dark hair, olive-toned skin, and the deepest brown eyes I'd ever seen, he was probably around our age, or maybe a little older.

"Hey, man," Hal said to him, sounding more casual than usual.

The boy had a pair of drumsticks sticking out the back pocket of his cargo pants, and some sheets of music in his hand. "Sorry, your dad let me in. I didn't know you were busy," he said, staring right at me, though he was talking to Hal.

In the side leg pocket of his pants was a book. I angled myself to see the title: *Letters to a Young Poet* by Rainer Maria Rilke. I must have read that at least eleven times.

Hal introduced the boy as West Kincaid, a junior at Endeavor, and the lead vocalist/part-time drummer/part-time bass player in their band. "This is the guy I was telling you about," Hal said to me. "The one who writes all our music."

"Nice to meet you," West said, still looking exclusively in my direction.

Even though he went to Endeavor, I was sure I'd never

seen him before. Wearing a plaid flannel scarf, and with a slight scruff on his chin, he embodied the definition of rock star.

Only better.

He smiled just a little, and I realized I was smiling, too. Hal looked back and forth between the two of us and cleared his throat, perhaps trying to break the sudden awkwardness in the room.

Because four had become a crowd.

My heart pounded and my palms pooled with sweat. "Have you read that book?" I asked West, nodding toward his pocket.

"Are you kidding? I'll read anything that'll make me a better writer. This one just happens to be my favorite."

"Are you a poet?"

"Some days I like to think I am. A poet and a song-writer."

"And other days?"

"Other days I guess I'm a student, trying to soak up as much as I can. Do you want to borrow it?" he asked, referring to the book.

"No, thanks. I've already read it."

"Oh, really," he said, more of a statement than a question, though still seemingly surprised. "It's pretty great, wouldn't you say? 'Go into yourself and test the deeps in which your life takes rise,'" he quoted.

"'At its source you will find the answer to the question

whether you *must* create,'" I continued. "'Accept it, just as it sounds, without inquiring into it.'"

"Cool," he said.

And, to be quite honest, I was sensing it, too—as corny as that notion may have sounded inside my head, I felt fantastic magnetism everywhere else. "Hal played me your song earlier. It was powerful," I told him, getting goose bumps all over just thinking about it.

"Really?" He smiled. "You liked it?"

Callie cleared her throat, echoing Hal from a few moments before. "So," she said, in an attempt to switch gears, "I thought there were only sophomores in the band . . . aside from Hal, that is."

West nodded, not fully paying attention. Instead he stayed focused on me, like I was the only person in the room.

"So, what's up?" Hal asked in an assertive tone, finally snapping West to attention.

West explained that he'd written some new lyrics, and he wanted Hal to check them out. "I also wrote notes to accompany them. So, play it and see what you think."

"Sounds good," Hal said.

"*Very* good." West gazed back at me.

A second later, Hal's mother sidled into the room again, clearing the magical tension in one fell swoop. Standing right behind her, to my complete and utter shock, was Beatrice Rossiter.

Practically straight from the hospital.

"Hal, you're not planning a party here tonight, are you? I think maybe we've reached our capacity. You kids want to move downstairs and I can get some snacks out or something?" his mother asked.

"I actually have to run anyway, dude," West told him. "Call me later?"

"Sure thing," Hal said. "I think we're okay, Mom. But thanks."

I waved good-bye to West just as Mrs. Bennett led Bea farther inside the room. "Callie, Nia, you both know Beatrice, right?" Mrs. Bennett asked.

Callie's mouth fell open in shock. Hal noticed, and tried to smooth things over by mentioning that Bea lived right across the street, and how great it was that she was finally out of the hospital. Mrs. Bennett left, still muttering about snacks and moving downstairs to a bigger space.

I didn't know whether to look at Bea or look at Callie. One night last winter, while Bea was walking home, Heidi pulled a hit-and-run. Bea was the victim. And instead of calling the police or helping Bea, Heidi drove straight to Callie's house, looking for an alibi.

Callie agreed, finally succumbing to Heidi's tears and threats. Luckily Beatrice survived the accident, but it left the entire side of her body disfigured, her face included. Somehow Amanda had uncovered the truth and she told Callie about it. Shortly after she'd disappeared, she left Callie a message that prompted her to do the right thing, which in turn stripped Callie of her VIP membership to the I-Girl Club.

Much to both her and our benefit, in the end.

Callie ended up alerting Heidi's mother to the whole ugly story. And though Mrs. Bragg denounced Callie and her family, the next thing everyone knew, some exclusive plastic surgeons at Johns Hopkins Hospital were donating their time and services to Bea's case.

Tonight the results were clear.

Bea looked stunning, as if the accident had never even happened. I'd almost forgotten how beautiful she was—how her skin was flawless, the color of milk chocolate; and how the sharp angles of her face were complemented by full lips and a pointed chin.

"You look amazing," Callie whispered breathlessly, tears in her eyes.

"Thank you," Bea said; her soft brown eyes crinkled up with her smile. "I'm still a little swollen." She motioned to the sides of her face. "And I'm wearing makeup to cover some of the bruising."

"Well, you'd never know it," I said, noticing right away that even her posture had changed—no longer slouched over, trying to hide herself. "It's good to see you looking so . . . you."

"Yeah, I'm excited to get back to school," Bea said. "To get back to normalcy again . . . despite Amanda's disappearance, that is. That's sort of why I'm here."

"What do you mean?" Hal asked.

"I mean, I hope you don't mind me barging in like this. It's just that I saw Nia get dropped off, and then I saw Callie pull up on her bike . . ."

I leaned forward, eager to know what she wanted to tell us.

"I know you guys have this Amanda Project thing going," she continued. "And I thought that maybe I could help." She reached into her jacket pocket and pulled out an envelope. "'You've got a friend,'" she said, reading the words printed neatly across the front in block lettering.

"Who gave that to you?" I asked eagerly.

"Good question. Someone left it for me at the hospital. I woke up in recovery and found it on my night table."

"Well, obviously it was a friend." Hal grinned, and then stopped when all eyes rolled.

"It might also be a song title," she said, proceeding to hum the James Taylor tune.

"I *love* that song," Callie cooed. "My parents used to dance to it in the living room when things were less—" She looked away, unable to finish the sentence.

Hal reached out to touch her shoulder in response.

Callie didn't talk about it much, but everybody knew anyway: Her mom had left her and her dad right around the time Amanda disappeared without so much as a good-bye note.

"There's more," Bea said. She opened the envelope and pulled out a rectangular card. It was a bit bigger than a playing card, and illustrated across the front was a lobster breaking through the surface of the ocean.

"It's from a tarot deck," she explained, handing the card to Callie. "I know because I researched it."

"It's old," Callie said, turning it over in her hand. The edges looked worn and yellow.

"It's probably an antique." Bea nodded. "Which is sort of significant on its own. You know . . . because Amanda really likes her antiques."

"So are you assuming that this is from her?" I asked.

"Who else?"

"Odds are—it could be from anyone," Callie said.

"Not likely." Hal shook his head. "I mean, we *are* talking about Amanda here: O Queen of Puzzling Gifts."

"They're actually not so puzzling when you stop to think about them," I argued, still wondering about Amanda and Bea's relationship. When Hal had broken in to Thornhill's computer for a second time—when he'd gotten to the page that had the mysterious coding and the list of names—he'd clicked on Bea's name and saw a black-and-white photo of her and Amanda together, wearing matching wigs and looking almost identical.

"So Amanda visited you at the hospital?" Callie asked Bea.

"I think so. I mean, I was out of it so much of the time. But I know what a fan she is of tarot art . . . at least, she told me she was. She used to talk about different illustrators she admired and collected certain cards."

"She *did*?" Hal asked, perhaps as surprised as I was. But then when I thought about it, it made perfect sense: Amanda admired all forms of art.

"Anyway, when I was doing all my research on the card," Bea continued, "I found that this particular one— with the lobster coming out of the water—symbolizes someone coming out of hiding."

"Well, she does come out of hiding." I nodded. "Every time she leaves us a clue."

"Maybe this is a sign that she plans to come out of hiding permanently," Bea guessed, unable to keep the sound of hope from her voice.

"How close are you and Amanda?" I asked, cutting straight to the chase.

Bea took a seat on Hal's bed. "She was always really nice to me. We had Spanish class together, and Amanda stuck up for me when Heidi and her I-Girl clones tortured me."

"*Tortured you?*" I asked, taking the card from Callie.

Bea hugged one of Hal's pillows. "Well, it feels like it. They would sit directly behind me and make fun of my style, saying it's *so* from the 1960s, and asking me where my bandana and tiny tinted sunglasses are . . . because I like tie-dye and hemp jewelry. They called me Beastly Bea, the hippie wannabe, and flashed me the peace sign . . . but in a really obnoxious, in-your-face sort of way."

I glanced over at Callie, who avoided my eye contact,

maybe because she'd heard some of these remarks before.

"It's pretty stupid," Bea said. "Like middle school times ten. But Amanda made it bearable. She sat beside me and wrote messages in the margins of her notebook . . . stuff like, 'Is it me, or does Heidi look extra orange today? Too much vitamin C? An accidental collision with a Sunkist truck maybe?' Because of her fake tan," Bea explained.

Callie let out a snicker.

"We also used to share favorite books, recommend music to each other, and discuss interesting quotes—the girl could quote from everywhere," Bea added. "It sounds lame when I try to describe it, but it really helped."

"So, you and Amanda were friends," I said to be sure.

Bea shrugged and looked back down at the envelope. "I guess you could call it that," she said, flashing me James Taylor's words. "But she did run a bit hot-and-cold sometimes, coming and going as she pleased, so I was never exactly sure of just where we stood."

"Yes, that sounds like Amanda." I nodded.

"Can we keep this card?" Hal asked.

"Sure," she said. "I figured you'd be able to scan it into your computer and add it to the website. I've been following the search there during my recovery."

I ran my fingers over the lobster's image, suddenly able to picture the card in Amanda's hand. I even saw her nail polish: a lemon and green blend of colors to go with the chunky topaz stone she often wore on her middle finger.

I closed my eyes and imagined her pulling the card

from the middle of one of her collaged notebooks, stuffing the card inside an envelope, and placing it on Bea's hospital table. I could see Bea all bandaged up and groggy, her eyelids barely peeping out from at least three layers of gauze and tape.

But the image quickly vanished when Hal plucked the card from my grip. "Cornelia will be so excited," he said, handing one of Cornelia's business cards to Bea. "She's trying to make a name for herself."

Part of me wanted to grab the tarot card back, to see if I could envision anything more. But another part was completely dumbfounded about why this was even happening to me—why I was sometimes able to touch an object and picture bits of its history.

"Do you remember anything specific about that night?" Callie asked Bea. "The night you were hit, I mean."

Hal and I exchanged a look, surprised that Callie was bringing it up.

"That's something else I wanted to talk to you about," Bea said slowly, looking at each of us in turn. "I was wearing Amanda's pink wig that night."

"While you were walking home?" I demanded, unable to contain myself.

She nodded. "I'd met Amanda at the library earlier. We were studying for a Spanish test. Heidi was there, too—not with us but at the next table over—and once again she was making fun of me, calling my braids all Woodstocky, and begging me to join the twenty-first century. Anyway, after Heidi had left, Amanda said she couldn't understand what Heidi was talking about—that my funky braids were way trendier than her wig. The next thing I knew, Amanda was taking off her wig and asking if I'd mind combing her hair out and putting a couple braids in to match mine. And so I did, but it felt weird being pseudo-twins . . . Frick and Frack."

"So, let me guess, you took the wig," I said.

Bea nodded. "I even wore it home that night."

I bit the inside of my cheek, remembering that fuchsia wig well. It was unmistakable with its twisty curls, bluntly cut bangs, and the way it cascaded down Amanda's back. "So, then, do you think you were mistaken for Amanda?" I asked, completely shocked.

"It's not like anyone else in Orion wears a wig like that." Hal automatically started drawing the wig in his sketchbook, his instant reaction in times of stress.

"But it's not like the car hit you on purpose, right?" I ventured, wondering if Bea ever saw Heidi's face.

And, while I expected Bea to deny the idea that someone hit her deliberately that night, she simply shrugged. "I honestly don't know," she said. "Maybe she hit me *because* she thought I was Amanda."

"*She?*" Callie asked, knowing the answer better than anyone, and perhaps wondering if Bea did, too.

"It was Heidi," she whispered. "After she hit me, she pulled over to see if I was dead. I remember lying on my side. Every bit of me was screaming in pain."

"Were you conscious?" I squeaked out, trying to focus on her answer.

"That's the tricky part. I mean, it was all so surreal: Heidi peeking out the window of a dark car, calling out Amanda's name, but then realizing that it was me. She seemed as startled as I was, almost scared."

I looked at Callie, eager to know, since Heidi had been driving her father's car that night, if Mr. Bragg's Beamer was indeed dark blue. But, from the look on Callie's face—eyes wide, lips parted, cheeks drained of all color—it clearly was.

"Why didn't you tell the police?" I asked.

"What makes you think that I didn't?" She wiped her tears on the corner of Hal's pillow. "I told the police what I saw. They came to talk to me at the hospital, but unfortunately the officer who questioned me was Heidi's own father. Chief Bragg told me I'd imagined the whole thing, that the medics said I wasn't conscious when they found me, and that it wasn't uncommon for trauma victims to enter dreamlike states before they fall unconscious."

"Then why bother questioning you at all?" Hal asked, shaking his head in frustration.

"Bragg asked me why I was biking by myself in the first place, if I'd been drinking or doing drugs and had stumbled out into the road as a result. I told him what I remembered about the accident, but he said that Heidi was with *him* that night."

"Excuse me?" Hal asked, glancing over at Callie.

"Apparently, he'd picked Heidi up at the library and took her out to dinner," Bea said. "They were sitting at the restaurant not thirty minutes before he got paged to come question me at the hospital."

"That's a lie," Callie blurted, clearly referring to the fact that Heidi had gone to *her* house that night, looking for an alibi. Little had Heidi known that her dad would be giving her an alibi, too.

I waited for Callie to elaborate, but when she didn't I scooted closer to Bea. I took her hand, grateful that she had survived, especially considering that Heidi was obviously much more lethal than any of us ever fathomed, and that as long as Officer Bragg was chief of police none of us would be safe.

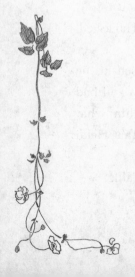

CHAPTER 16

At school the following day, I just couldn't get everything Bea had told us out of my head. Seeing Heidi swanning down the hallways now—and in classes, in the cafeteria, applying a fresh coat of lipstick at her locker mirror—took on a whole new edge, because I couldn't help but wonder: Did she really have the potential to kill?

Needless to say, we never did get to the pharmacy that night. After Bea left, it was all we could do not to tear Hal's bedroom to shreds. That's how angry we were. And how desperate we felt.

And so during trig class, I gave myself little tests. I found myself touching various objects, looking for answers—from Stew Loicamar's dropped pencil to the hood of Tanya Rosegrey's sweater when she draped it over her chair.

But I felt nothing. And I pictured even less.

Completely frustrated, I pulled Bea's tarot card from my backpack. I'd managed to pocket it before I left Hal's last night, promising to return it later today so that Cornelia could add it to the website. I slid my fingertips over the card's edges, suddenly able to visualize it perfectly in Amanda's hands.

Only this time she wasn't in the hospital. I was picturing her on a different day—Amanda had different nail polish (plum) and she was wearing a big ruby stone on her index finger.

In my mind's eye, I could see her in a tiny, eclectic book shop—just like the one I'd seen when I touched my edition of *Ariel*. She was sitting in a red velvet chair, reading an old copy of *The Adventures of Huckleberry Finn* by Mark Twain. When she was finished with her page, she tucked the tarot card into the book as a placeholder.

"Nia?" Mrs. Watson's sharp voice interrupted. She was squatted, one seat back, in the row beside mine, checking over Muriel Spencer's polynomials. "Do you have a question?"

"No, ma'am," I said, slipping the card beneath my notebook so she couldn't see it.

"So, then, do you always talk to yourself for no apparent reason?" she asked.

A sprinkling of giggles erupted in the classroom.

"I was thinking out loud," I corrected her. "It's hard to concentrate with all the chattering going on." And I wasn't just referring to *her* chattering as she worked with students. I was also talking about the whispering going on at the rear of the classroom, where Darryl Coppersmith and Goofball Gus were comparing the stench of each other's breath by exhaling on graph paper. "Since we're working independently today, would you mind if I took the rest of the block at the library?" It wasn't as if I hadn't gotten all of my word problems right within the first ten minutes of class. I'd even finished the assignments for the next three nights, including some extra credit exercises I'd thrown in out of sheer boredom.

"Fine," she said, after a five-second pause, unable to come up with a good reason to deny my request.

I hurried out of class and headed to the library, eager to start researching antique book shops in Orion. There were two: a large one with its own website with clickable links, and another nameless one by the train station—nameless, because it was merely called Antiques. Semi-anonymous and obscure: I assumed that was the one.

I'd seen it many times before, but had never actually gone inside. I scrolled down over the snapshot image on the computer, remembering everything I'd pictured when I touched my copy of *Ariel*: the tiny, frail man who worked the front desk, the calculator and notepad he used to record the day's sales, and the random trinkets lined up on dusty shelves.

I was relieved when the bell rang to switch classes, when I could finally get to the cafeteria to tell Hal and Callie what I'd seen.

"A velvet chair?" Callie asked, pausing from her yogurt to give me a puzzled stare.

"*Mark Twain?*" Hal made a face. "That doesn't exactly sound like Amanda. Isn't she more into modern-day poetry and Gothic fiction?"

"She likes *all* literature," I corrected him, "including classics, which definitely includes Twain. Plus, what happened to pursuing any and all leads we get? We need to go to that bookstore."

"We also need to go to the pharmacy and the airstrip," he said. "I think those are our priorities."

"They are all priorities," I snapped.

"Let's say for the sake of argument that what you pictured was indeed a real scene involving Amanda," Hal said, letting his plastic fork drop. "What makes you think you've got the right antique shop?"

"I don't just *think*," I insisted, correcting him. "I *know*. I'm confident. It's the right shop."

"So?" Callie asked, seeming confused. "Not that two plus two always has to equal four, but where are you going with this?"

"I'm not sure. But she left the card, and I touched it, and now I'm seeing her there . . . I just want to pursue this and see where it takes us. So, anyone up for skipping our next period? The shop is only a five-minute ride away." I showed them the address scribbled on my palm. "We'll be back before the bell even rings."

"What's the rush?" Callie asked. "I mean, I'm just nervous about cutting classes. I can only get us out of so many detentions."

"Especially if Amanda had the tarot card with her *at* the bookshop," Hal said. "I mean, if what you pictured is actually correct, she'd have gone to that shop even *before* she went to visit Bea at the hospital. So she would be long gone by now."

"Look, it's not that I'm one for taking skipping classes lightly," I told them. "But I just feel like we're running out of time here, and we still have so many places left to investigate. Meanwhile Amanda remains missing, potentially in danger."

"You have to look at this from our perspective," Hal continued. "You touched a card, which conjured up an image of something that supposedly happened at least a week ago—"

"I know it sounds crazy," I interrupted him, wondering why he was being so narrow-minded, especially considering how many of his harebrained hunches we'd followed in the past. "But maybe she left us a clue at that shop. Maybe we could talk to the shop owner, or search for that copy of *Huck Finn* . . ."

"We'll find Amanda," he promised. "But we're not going to be able to do it within the next sixty minutes. I have an essay due next period."

I ignored him by taking an extra-large bite of my mother's homemade pasta, making it hard to talk. We barely said anything about Amanda for the rest of our lunch period together. We barely even spoke at all.

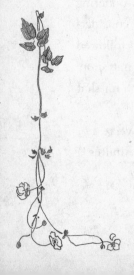

CHAPTER 17

I tried to concentrate during the next couple of periods, tried to listen to Mr. Randolph lecture on about the post–Civil War Industrialization Movement, and tried not to drop dead of boredom while Madame Booté reviewed—again—the rules of *le subjonctif* for the unenlightened.

But I honestly couldn't stop thinking about Amanda—about the possibility that she might've left us a clue at that bookstore.

And so instead of going to the library for my last free period, I slipped out the side exit door behind the cafeteria. The door was open anyway; the janitors had been cleaning out a storage closet and making trips out to the Dumpster. I cut across the back parking lot, grabbed my bike, and rode into town, relieved to finally be doing the right thing.

About five minutes later, I pulled up in front of the antique bookshop—a tiny shack of a place. The OPEN sign was hanging crookedly in the window, and yet it looked dark inside.

I parked my bike and tried the door. It opened with a loud and whining creak. The inside of the shop smelled like a mix of mildew and cigar smoke. Still, it was just as I imagined. Books lined the walls on old and splintery shelves. A long center table served as a display for antique trinkets like candle holders and chunky costume jewelry. And there was an old, fragile-looking man there, too. He had to have been at least eighty years old, with a hearing aid behind one ear and a distinctive curve to his spine.

"Good day," he said, looking at me from behind a pair of tiny bifocals.

He was just as I'd imagined, too, as was his desk. It wasn't a conventional counter with a cash register, but instead a metal folding table with a calculator and notepad.

"Can I help you with something?" he wheezed.

"Not just yet," I told him, eager to poke around on my own.

The man shrugged and went about his business, calculating a bunch of receipt totals. Meanwhile, I moved farther into the shop, nearly tripping over a ceramic statue of a crouching little lion.

A moment later, I saw it—the red velvet chair. I

approached it slowly, noticing a stack of books on the table beside it. One of them was *The Adventures of Huckleberry Finn* by Mark Twain.

My fingers trembled as I picked it up. I thumbed through the pages, able to picture Amanda standing at the front of the shop with the book tucked under her arm, contemplating a pair of emerald teardrop earrings, and then slipping a note of some sort between a couple of books on a shelf. Exciting as that was, I wanted to check in with the shopkeeper first.

I approached his desk. "Do you remember a girl coming in here recently? She'd be about my age, and she might've been sitting in that red velvet chair, reading a copy of *Huck Finn*?"

He thought about it for several long seconds before nodding his head. "Eh, yep. She might've been about your age."

"And do you know anything about her?" I asked, feeling my pulse race. "Where she might be staying, or how often she comes in here? Did she say anything you remember?"

He chuckled. "I know I've seen that girl with so many different hairstyles: short and black one day, long and blond the next. I get dizzy keepin' track of all her wigs."

"So she comes in here often?"

"Often?" He tapped his shiny bald head in thought.

"When was the last time she was in here?"

"Well, that would have been a week or so ago, at least. She comes in here because she says she likes the smell of old books. She sits in that there chair"—he nodded toward the velvet one—"and reads for a good while."

"Is there anything else you can tell me? Any particular books she favors?" I asked, wondering if there was a clue in one of the titles.

The man thought about it for a couple moments, scratching at the scruff on his chin with his fingernails. "Come to think of it . . . a few weeks back, she'd asked me to find a particular edition of a book. And, you know, we offer that service free of charge so long as you purchase the book once I find it."

"Which book?" I asked, practically jumping over the table and cutting him off.

"*Ariel,*" he said. "By Sylvia Plath. I remember she wanted a first-edition copy. You know how rare that is? I told her it would cost her, but she didn't seem to care. She said it was a gift for a special friend."

"It was *my* gift," I told him, plunking down on the floor. "It was for me."

He nodded, pausing a moment to eye me over, as if maybe he knew something more. "Well, if you're ever anxious to sell it back . . ."

"Do you know where Amanda lives . . . or where she might be staying?" I asked him again. "Did she give you any contact information as to how you could reach her once you'd found the copy of *Ariel*?"

"Amanda?" he asked, seemingly caught on the name. "That's not right, is it?" He made a confused face.

"Maybe she went by something else?" I asked.

He gazed at one of those old-fashioned cat clocks—the kind that has the shifty eyes and the tail that tick-tocks back and forth. "My, if it isn't two o'clock already . . . I think I might need to take a little break." He removed his bifocals and rubbed at his eyes. "Sometimes my mind starts going a little wackadoo when I'm trying to keep track of all these details."

"Please," I insisted. "I really need your help. Amanda is missing. People all over town are looking for her."

The man ignored me, picking up his stack of receipts. He slipped his glasses back on and resumed his calculations, as if I weren't even there—as if taking a little break meant doing anything other than talking to me.

I moved toward the exit, catching a glimpse of a RARE BOOKS sign on the wall. It pointed to a short shelf of books. There were copies of old editions of *Alice's Adventures in Wonderland*, *The Scarlet Letter*, and even a signed copy of Stephen King's *Christine*. I ran my fingers over the bindings as I searched, my eyes stopping at the P section, where a pair of emerald teardrop earrings had been mislaid, just as I'd envisioned moments ago.

"Amanda," I whispered, almost tempted to try them on. Instead I took a deep breath, and resumed looking for books by Plath, for where a copy of *Ariel* might've been kept.

And that's where I found it. Amanda's note. Stuffed between two books. It was a poem, handwritten in her distinctive penmanship:

Shattered

The rock's been thrown.
The window is broken.
Shards of glass have torn through your walls of trust.
Do not think I am unaware that your perception of me.
Is shattered.
But one day.
In time.
I hope.
We can clean up this glass.
And mend the window.
And ease open the pane.
To look beyond what has broken.
To see what truly lies on the inside.
Only then can shattered glass ever be replaced.

My heart pounded just reading the words—just knowing Amanda wrote them. Below the poem was a tiny sketch of a coyote, Amanda's totem, the trickster.

"Can I help you?" the shopkeeper asked once more. He stood up from his desk and looked to see what I was doing. "What have you got there?" he asked.

"Nothing. And thank you. I'm fine." I folded the poem back up, stuffed it inside my coat, and left without another word.

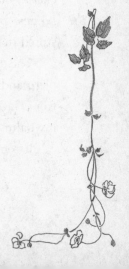

CHAPTER 18

I raced back to school just as kids were filing out for the day, and rode around to the side parking lot, hoping that I hadn't missed Callie or Hal.

Both of them were there, unlocking their bikes from the rack. I started in their direction, but then spotted a car pulling up beside them. It was an Alfa Romeo—a classic one from the 1970s in almost mint condition. I knew because my father used to keep one just like it stored in our garage.

The driver cranked the window open, and to my complete and utter surprise, it was West, the junior I'd met from Hal's band. He and Hal exchanged some words. And my palms instinctively pooled with sweat.

It took at least a couple of minutes, but I worked up

the nerve to say hello. Only before I got there, West drove away, leaving me in the Land of If-Only. Population: 1.

I grabbed Amanda's note in my pocket, reminding myself of my priorities, and then I made a beeline for the bike rack.

"Hey, where did *you* come from?" Hal asked, spotting me just behind him.

"The bookshop," I told him, unfolding Amanda's poem and handing it over. "What can I say? I went with my instinct, and it proved correct. I will accept apologies for the lack of confidence later."

Callie and Hal took a few moments to read the poem over. "Is it me," Callie asked, "or does the point of this poem seem uncharacteristically clear?"

"Definitely." I nodded. "Amanda wants us to find out the truth about her, but at the same time she's feeling a bit guilty."

"Guilty because our perception of her has been shattered," Hal said slowly.

"But it's not like she didn't have reason to lie. I mean, right?" Callie asked.

"I don't know," Hal said. "I think I could've done without some of those bogus stories. I just wish she'd have trusted me enough to be honest."

"Except she wasn't necessarily lying to protect *herself*," I reminded them. "She was also trying to protect *us*."

"And one day she hopes to rebuild our trust." A tiny smile of relief curled across Callie's lips.

This was exactly what all of us needed: Amanda acknowledging her web of lies, concerned about what we might think of her, because she truly valued our friendships.

"Still, I just have one question," Hal began, focused on me. "How did Amanda know you'd go to that shop? The only reason you did was because you touched a tarot card and a picture popped into your mind."

"Right," Callie said. "Plus, how did Amanda even know that Bea gave you that card?"

"For all we know, Amanda *told* Bea to give us the card," I said. "Who knows if Bea was giving us the whole story?"

"So, do you actually believe that Amanda assumed you would go immediately to investigate an antique book place because you handled a tarot card?" Callie wondered, looking at me.

I shook my head, completely puzzled over it all myself.

Hal paused a moment to look at me—to really gaze into my eyes, making me feel suddenly self-conscious. "If I didn't know better, I'd think that maybe *you* were hiding something."

"Like you did with the *Ariel* book," Callie ventured.

"And like *you* did with Bea's accident," I reminded

her, thinking how Amanda hadn't been the only one to keep secrets. When it came to the subject of secret-keeping, we were all a little more like Amanda than we wanted to admit.

"I assure you," I said finally, "I'm not hiding any-thing—not anymore. I honestly have no idea how or why Amanda assumed I'd go there."

"Here," Hal said, handing the poem back to me. "Do you picture anything when you touch this?"

"No," I said, holding it longer to be sure.

"Books, plot plans, necklace charms, tarot cards . . ." Callie rubbed at the ache in her head. "I mean, talk about random . . . the objects you're able to envision stuff from, that is."

"I'm sorry I can't be more accommodating," I said sharply. "And what's *your* superpower?"

Callie ignored me and pulled a small, well-worn sea-shell coin purse from her bag. "Try this," she said, wanting me to touch it.

I ran my fingers over it. "Sorry," I said, giving it back to her, frustrated.

"So, maybe your power only works when the object is Amanda-related," Hal said.

I shook my head, confident that wasn't the case, thinking about the time I touched my grandfather's old military hat or, more recently, Heidi's phone.

"Maybe Amanda is able to envision things about you,

too," Hal offered, still focused on me. "Maybe *that's* how she knew you'd eventually go to the bookstore."

"Who knows?" I told them. "But we won't get anywhere standing in this parking lot. Let's go investigate that pharmacy once and for all."

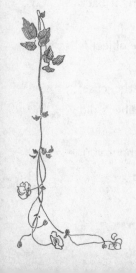

CHAPTER 19

We rode to the pharmacy with me taking the lead. On the way there, we stopped several times to examine the serpent-and-bowl markings on various buildings, including the bank, the post office, and the old courthouse. But, not surprisingly, none of them had the infamous onyx eye.

After about ten minutes of pedaling, we finally arrived in front of the tall brick building that Amanda and I had visited.

"Well, I can certainly see what you meant," Callie offered. "This does sort of look like an apartment complex. I've passed by this place a bunch of times, but never in a million years thought it was a pharmacy."

I peered up toward the serpent-and-bowl marking, noticing immediately that the eye had been taken out. I moved through the gate and up the front stairs for a closer look, convinced I was able to spot a bit of the residual adhesive in which the eye had originally been set.

"So, shall we go in?" Callie asked, stepping toward the door. She jiggled the knob, but it didn't budge. "Locked."

"Hold on," I said, remembering that when Amanda and I had come here we waited a couple minutes before someone finally let us in.

Callie pounded on the door with her fist. "Are you sure this is the place? Oh, right, the serpent." She nodded.

I looked up at the windows to try to detect movement or light, suspecting that if the onyx was gone, the business inside would be, too.

Finally, the door opened. "Can I help you?" a woman asked. Wearing a navy-blue suit and holding a clipboard, she had coarse black hair held back in a twist, but on second glance it almost looked like a wig.

"We're looking for Waverly Valentino," I said.

"Sorry, but I can't help you," she said, barely glancing up from her notes.

"Then could we buy some tea?" Callie ventured.

The woman gave us a confused look, her eyebrows knitting together. "I think you might be confused. This building is being put up for lease. I'm the Realtor, assessing its merits. We should have a sign outside, along with some listing sheets, by tomorrow."

"What kind of property is it?" Hal asked.

"Are you interested, young man?" She smirked.

"No . . . but my parents might be."

She eyed him up and down, as if trying to determine his honesty. "This place has a lot of potential," she said, her voice throaty and deep. "It could be used as apartments, a small business, or private school . . . There's even potential for a multifamily."

"Or a pharmacy?" I asked, still fishing for information.

The woman cocked her head, almost bemused.

"What *was* this place?" Hal asked her. "Before the last lease ran out, I mean."

"Apartments, mostly."

"*Mostly?*" I asked.

"I'm assuming," she said. "It was vacant during the walk-through. And my boss said the owners of the property are rather private, so she couldn't really give me specifics. Apparently there's some confidential history tied to the property, and the owners would like things handled discreetly."

"Can you tell us the owners' names?" Callie asked.

"Not in this case. Everything's being kept under lock and key, so to speak." She chuckled at her own lame joke.

"*Everything?*" I asked.

"It's rare, but it happens. And we have to respect the owners' wishes. *We work for you at Ryder Realty*," she said, punching out the slogan. She gestured to her Ryder Realty pin: a gold-plated house logo on the lapel of her jacket. "But I thank you for your interest." She flashed us a plastic Realtor smile—complete with pearly veneers and sheer pink lipstick—and then turned away.

"Wait," I said, eager to ask her more.

"Of course," she said, turning back and reaching into her pocket. She handed Hal her business card: "My name is Whitney Vanderman. Have your parents give me a call if they're interested. But don't wait too long, or else you'll wind up missing."

My mouth dropped open in shock. *Excuse me?* I asked.

"You won't know what you're missing," the woman said; a bewildered expression hung on her face, like she had no idea what my problem was. "Three floors, separate heating units, a brand-new boiler system, and central air to boot," she continued. "Properties like this don't come along often. I'll give it two days on the market—tops."

"Thanks," Hal said, taking the card.

The woman wished us a good afternoon and then closed the door behind her.

"I don't think she's lying," Hal said, showing us her Realtor card.

"Agreed," Callie said. "She didn't seem sketchy at all."

"Even when she said that we might 'wind up missing'?" I asked.

"Wait, *what*?" Hal's face contorted in confusion.

"I heard it, too," Callie said. "But I think it must've been a slip of the tongue."

"So, what now?" I asked. "Should we call this woman and pretend to be interested in the property? Insist on knowing its history, and where the preexisting pharmacy moved to before we agree to buy it? And hey, anyone else notice that the real estate agent and Waverly Valentino share the same initials?"

"Whoa. Can that be a coincidence? I mean, I guess it could. But it doesn't sound like she knows anything about a pharmacy," Callie said. "And even if she does, it's not like she or her boss would tell us."

"You don't seriously think they closed up shop just because of our phone call, do you?" I asked.

"I don't know," Hal said. "But maybe we should try calling that Waverly woman again—on the off chance that we *did* catch her at a bad time before. Maybe she'll be more willing to talk. When did you come here before, anyway? Could the pharmacy have been gone for a while?"

"I suppose." I thought about it. "It was probably a few months ago."

He made a universal phone call signal with his outstretched fingers. "Let's give this call another go."

I nodded and took a seat on the front steps. Callie and Hal sat beside me. I blocked my number, set the mode to speakerphone, and then I dialed her.

The phone rang, and I felt my heart tighten.

Four rings. Five.

"Not such a good sign. Nobody picking up," Callie noted, drumming her fingers.

After the ninth ring, the phone finally made a click

sound. A recording came on, informing us that the number had been disconnected, and that no further information was available.

"So, this was indeed the place," I said, still wondering about the sunflower clue.

"I really think we need to check out that airstrip next," Hal said. "We're running out of clues."

"Tomorrow," I agreed. "We'll go to the airstrip after school. It's a half day."

"Sounds good," Callie said, checking her watch. "But right now I have to go."

We said good-bye, and then each started to race off on our separate ways to meet our curfews, but before I could even reach the end of the street, I felt myself come to a sudden halt.

Right in front of me, spray-painted on the side of the gas station building, was a giant sunflower.

I quickly turned back to see where Hal and Callie had gone, but unfortunately neither of them was anywhere in sight.

CHAPTER 20

At home that evening, my mother and I were in the kitchen, chopping garlic and mincing onion, absorbed in our ritual of preparing my father's favorite empanadas, when the kettle whistle sounded, announcing that Dad's tea was ready. "Would you mind bringing your father his chai?" Mama asked, eyes runny from the onion.

"Sure," I said, adding not *one*, not *two*, but exactly one and a half sugar cubes to the cup—precisely the way he liked it. We are a particular family, the Riveras. One and all. I stirred it up well and then took the tea to the living room, where he had a coaster already set out.

"Thank you, Nia *a mi corazón*," he said, barely looking up from the sports section of the daily paper. "What time is dinner tonight?"

"I think Mama said seven, just after Cisco gets home from soccer."

"Let me guess: auction committee meeting?" Finally he folded down a corner of the paper and smiled at me.

I smiled, too. There was something about my father's face, particularly when he was smiling—the crinkle of his dark eyes, perhaps, or the way his cheeks formed deep dimples—that always made everything feel a little better.

I watched him take a sip of chai, wondering how someone as noble and respected as he could possibly be involved in anything as shady as that list.

Unless maybe he didn't even know about the list. And maybe he'd never seen the photo of Thornhill beneath the vase.

But was my mother capable of keeping such big secrets?

A second later the doorbell rang. I crossed the living room to answer it, figuring it must be a UPS delivery or a FedEx package for my father. But when I looked through the peephole, I was absolutely stunned.

Because Keith Harmon was there.

Keith Harmon—who I'd barely even spoken to since that whole mortifying debacle in middle school, who was no longer even a speck on my proverbial radar now, but who somehow still managed to cause the slightest of stings whenever I saw him.

What could he possibly want?

I reluctantly opened the door. Keith waved when he saw me, and mouthed a "Hey" through the door glass. I looked toward the back of my father's head, a good twenty feet away. And then I opened the door to invite Keith inside.

"Hey, Nia. Do you have a second?" Keith asked. He was standing in the front entryway now.

Dad glanced in my direction and then stood from the sofa when he saw Keith. Apparently my father did not like what he saw. He has impeccable instincts, that man. "Is everything okay, Nia?" he asked, taking an extra moment to stare Keith down.

"Keith is just a friend from school," I said. A blatant lie.

Dad nodded the chilly hello he seemed to reserve for boys and then reluctantly sat back down.

"What can I do for you?" I asked Keith, wondering if this was yet another I-Girl plot.

Keith scratched at the back of his neck and shuffled his feet a couple of times, seemingly as uncomfortable as I was. "Wow. Awkward." He let out what I guessed was a nervous laugh. Still, his dark gray eyes scanned my face, as if surprised by what he saw—almost like he didn't know me anymore, like he'd forgotten who I was.

Just like he *had* forgotten before.

He forgot that time in the sixth grade, when Ms. MacKenzie, our art teacher, had us re-create the scene from Matisse's painting *The Dance*. A group of us stood in a circle, holding hands, doing our best to sway in our ring-around-the-rosy-type dance.

Keith and I had been holding hands, and at one point he tripped over his feet, and toppled right onto me. We ended up in a tray of purple paint. Ms. MacKenzie was not amused, but Keith and I couldn't stop laughing—so hard that my stomach ached. Keith managed to giggle out an apology, and I accepted by painting a line down his face with my finger. He did the same—only instead of a line down my face, it was a giant heart on my cheek.

And suddenly things weren't funny anymore. Of course, he managed to forget all that the next year.

"What do you want?" I asked him, wondering if he ever thought back to that day when I sat in the cafeteria waiting for him, only to be ridiculed by the whole lunchroom. Or if he ever thought back to art class in sixth grade . . .

"Well, I actually have something to give you, if that's okay." He pulled a box from his pocket and held it out.

I took it, almost expecting it to be part of a joke. I opened the lid and removed a layer of tissue.

Inside was a black onyx stone—just like the one placed in the eyes of the serpents around town. Also inside was a tiny wooden tile from an old board game. I picked up the tile and flipped it over in my palm. The word CAREFUL was printed across the front, and a picture of a coyote had been stamped onto the back.

My heart pounded. "Where did you get this?" I demanded.

"I found it," he said. "On my windowsill. When I got up this morning."

"And do you know who it was from?"

"There was just a note attached." He shrugged. "But it said that I should give this to you."

I shook my head, knowing there had to be a lot more to it. Why else would he bother giving it to me? Why wouldn't he simply throw it away in the trash and forget that it ever existed? Why potentially embarrass himself by coming to my house?

"Where *is* the note?"

"Gone." He shrugged again. "I pitched it."

My face flashed red, because I knew that he was lying. "What does Amanda have on you?" I asked him, keeping my voice low. "Do you two have a past that I don't know about?"

"Nia?" my father asked, turning to gaze back at us.

"Everything's fine," I told him. "We're just trying to determine the best argument for a Mock UN debate."

"Um. What makes you think this is about *Amanda*?" Keith asked me, lowering his voice now, too. "I didn't say anything about that chick."

"I *know* it's about her," I said, correcting him. Why else would Keith, of all people, have been chosen to give me this warning?

Keith folded his arms and stuck out his chest—a move I'd seen him do before, especially with I-Girls. "You've changed a lot this year, haven't you?" he said, giving me the once-over. "It's like you're a totally different person."

"You're right," I agreed, remembering how Louise had

mentioned it, too. Fashion and makeup aside, I was no longer the same girl.

And I had Amanda to thank for that.

"Well, thank you for the delivery. I will take it from here." I was fairly certain it was pretty useless trying to get more information out of him. I nodded to the door, but Keith suddenly seemed less than enthusiastic to leave.

"You know there's a cool new café in town," he started. "Everybody's saying they make the best mochaccinos around. Want to try it out one day?"

"I like coffee," I said coldly. "But not nearly that much." And with that, I opened the door wide and kicked him to the curb.

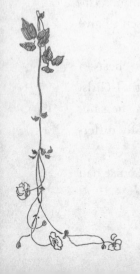

CHAPTER 21

School on Friday went by in a blur, mostly because everyone was so excited about the talent show that night. No
one was really paying much attention in classes, including Mr. Richards. He kept going on about the stand-up
routine he was going to do, using us as the guinea pigs
for his George Carlin–wannabe one-liners.

I made an honest effort to laugh in all the right places,
especially since I was grateful to skip track exercises as a
reward. It gave me more time to chart our afternoon's
activities

By noon dismissal time, I was more than ready to
leave. And so when the early release bell finally rang, I
think I literally was the first person out the door. But
I wasn't exactly the only anxious one. Hal and Callie
weren't even two minutes behind me. When they got to

me, I was sitting on my bike.

"How do you always do that?"

"What?" I said, raising an eyebrow in a move I stole from Ali McGraw.

"Nothing."

"Never mind. Are we ready?" Hal sighed.

"Not quite," I said, pulling Keith's gift box from my pocket. I showed them both the onyx stone and the wooden tile, explaining Keith Harmon's visit.

"A warning from Amanda," Hal said, pointing out the coyote stamp on the back of the tile.

"Definitely. But you and Keith aren't exactly friends," Callie said, stating the obvious. "So why would he bother doing what this missing *note* instructed?"

"That was my question, too," I told her.

"Unless maybe he *wants* to be friends," she wondered, winking at me. "I mean, you *have* been looking pretty smokin' lately."

"I have a much more likely theory," I said, glaring at her. "I think Amanda has something on him. Something really scandalous."

"Okay. But then why play that scandal card *now*?" Callie asked. "And with *you*. I mean, she could've had any-one deliver that gift."

"And she could've had Keith deliver it to either of us," Hal added.

"Right, but she chose to have Keith Harmon deliver the message to me," I said, still slowly puzzling about that, as I had since last night.

"Maybe because she wanted you to have closure from what happened in middle school," Callie said softly, clearly trying to step carefully around my feelings.

"Nice theory, but I don't need closure," I snapped. "What happened in middle school is yesterday's news."

"Well, maybe Amanda didn't think so," she continued. "Maybe Amanda felt like you needed to face Keith in order to move on . . . to something or someone . . ."

I looked away, hating to admit it—because I'd truly believed that I was over what happened in middle school—but it actually *had* felt liberating to face Keith. And once again, I had Amanda to thank. I gave Callie a sheepish smile, silently acknowledging that she was right.

"So, the gift was obviously a warning," Hal said, studiously avoiding our exchange. "I mean, 'careful' with the onyx eye. More than unusual, right? She must know we've been snooping around those buildings."

"And she must know that we're getting dangerously close," I agreed.

"So, what do you say we get a little closer?" Hal grinned, grabbing Cornelia's MapQuest directions from his bag. "Are we ready?"

"I was ready yesterday," I told him.

"Me too," Callie chirped.

We set out on our bikes for the long ride. At least fifteen minutes after we'd entered the town of Saint Claude by way of Blackbird Avenue, things were starting to look pretty rural—as in *Little House on the Prairie* rural: tall grass, wide pastures, lots of farmland, and abandoned-looking structures.

"Are you sure this is the right way?" Callie called out.

But it made perfect sense that an airstrip would be in a remote location. We pedaled down a long dirt road. A grassy field stretched out on one side of us, while what looked like a wooded conservation lot was on the other.

Finally we reached it: a sign that read CASTEEL MILITARY AIRSTRIP was staked into the ground. A barbed wire fence surrounded the property, and an unoccupied guard shack stood just beyond the locked gate.

The airstrip was mostly vacant except for a hangar and a tanker truck, both at opposite ends of the property. I peered past a NO TRESPASSING sign. The hangar was exactly as I'd pictured: a giant steel building with dark blue stripes that ran along the front and side walls.

"Okay, there is the small matter of how we get in," Callie said, gesturing to a thick chain threaded through and around the opening. A padlock held it in place.

I continued to scope the hangar out, wondering where the security guards were.

Hal decided to check the lock. He twisted and pulled at it, trying to get it to budge. The muscles in his arms flexed as he strained. He even smashed it repeatedly with a large rock. Still it didn't open, despite how old and rusty it looked. Callie walked a ways, looking for any downed trees to act as ladders and weak spots in the fence.

I placed my foot against the gate, applying pressure as I leaned my weight forward. Gripping the bottom corner of the gate, I tried to bend it upward—just enough—so that we might be able to slip underneath. Hal attempted to help me, but even together we couldn't get the gate to give.

"We could always scale the fence," he said, all out of breath.

"Are you kidding?" Callie asked, back from surveying the fence. "That's got to be at least twelve feet high. Not to mention the fact that I really don't feel like becoming a barbed wire ornament."

"We'll throw a jacket over the wire." He pulled a Swiss Army knife from his back pocket and poked the point of the nail file into the lock. He jiggled it back and forth in a final attempt. But that didn't work either.

"Let *me* try. You guys don't know my past as an international jewel thief," she joked. Callie grabbed the file right out of his hand and squatted down in front of the lock. Hal and I huddled up to conceal her. After a few seconds spent trying to finagle the lock open with the file, she threw the knife down and tried to pull the chain apart.

With her hands.

I couldn't help but roll my eyes at the sight of Callie in her baby-doll dress and ballet flats, manhandling the steel links. Still, her arms pulsed, every bit as taut as Hal's.

Callie let out a groan as she worked to pull two of the rustier links apart. Finally, the chain broke. Callie fell backward, glancing off the fence and losing her balance from the blow. She DID it.

"How is that possible? Are you suddenly some kind of Amazon?" I asked, helping her up.

Hal managed a small smile, but it was clear that he was completely bewildered, too.

"I don't know," she said, shocked. "I guess I didn't realize how determined I was." She peered down at her small, slender hands, suddenly noticing a cut about five inches long.

Blood ran down her arm where a sharp corner of the fence had torn right through her skin.

I unwound my scarf from my neck and used it as a tourniquet around her arm. Meanwhile, Hal moved closer to see if he could help, offering his bottled water to clean the cut.

Most people would have been reeling in pain, but Callie waved us off: "I'm fine, really," she said, eager to keep going. She got up and blotted the blood with the scarf's slack. "And I'll pay for your dry cleaning."

"Who cares about the scarf," I told her. "As long as you're okay."

"Definitely okay, honestly," she said, clearly not wanting to make a fuss. "Let's crack this place."

"Wait, did you guys just hear something?" Hal turned his head and held his hand up, looking all around us.

"Hear what?" I asked, unable to detect much more than the whirring wind and the sound of our own breathing.

"Nothing." He was still for a minute and then shook

his head and went for the chain again. He unthreaded it from the gate's opening. "We're in."

Before we headed to the hangar, we stashed our bikes behind a clump of bushes several yards from the entrance. Hal closed the gate behind us, and we hurried across the airstrip—probably about as wide as our high school parking lot. We ducked behind some oil drums, just a few feet away from the open garage door.

"What now?" Callie wondered.

Before we could answer, Hal snuck from around the side of the drums and went inside the hangar. "Come on," he whispered, squatting down behind a set of stairs on wheels (the kind the airlines use to get people on board) just inside the doorway.

Callie and I joined him. The hangar looked mostly empty except for some storage boxes, a luggage carrier, and a dark green convertible Jeep parked on the opposite side. I stood up to venture out a little farther. At the same moment, Callie grabbed hold of my sleeve, and I quickly ducked back down.

There was a man sitting at a desk only a few yards away, to the side of us. He was completely slumped over, almost flush with the top of the desk. His head was down, resting on the pages of a book.

"Shhh," Hal hissed. "He's sleeping."

Dressed in a dark uniform, he was some sort of a security person, although fairly incompetent, obviously. A golf cart was parked beside him.

A second later, an engine roared. The sound echoed across the building and woke the security guard. His head jerked up, feigning alertness.

It took me a second to realize where the sound was coming from. The Jeep pulled forward with a screech. Its bright lights shined in my eyes, nearly rendering me blind. At first I thought the Jeep was coming right for us, but instead it stopped just shy of our hiding place.

We remained crouched behind the set of stairs. My heart was pounding so hard I was sure they could hear it, too.

"Is everything okay?" the security guard called out.

The driver, some guy wearing a red bandana, responded with a wave. Another gruff-looking guy with a tattoo on his cheek—I couldn't really make out the design—was talking on a cell phone, but his voice was too muffled to hear.

"Keep low," Hal whispered, pulling Callie down. Blood dripped from under the scarf onto the ground.

Still, I kept focused on the Jeep. There was an older man, probably in his seventies, sitting in the passenger seat. He looked much different than the other two men—less confident, more scared. Definitely out of his element.

The security guard hopped into his golf cart. I held my breath, waiting for all of them to leave, wondering what the holdup was and if they'd seen us.

Finally, the Jeep drove away with a screech, out the hangar door opening. The security guard's back to me, I inched my head out a little farther, noticing that the Jeep wasn't heading for the main gate—probably toward the tanker truck.

"We don't belong here," Callie whispered.

"Well, we're not leaving now," I said, checking for the security guard. A walkie-talkie strapped to his belt, he did a full lap around the interior of the hangar before finally heading outside.

Our cue to scope things out.

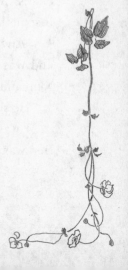

CHAPTER 22

We hurried across the airline hangar in search of anything
that would give us a clue as to Amanda's whereabouts.
There had to be a connection. While Callie rifled through
the folders on the security guard's desk, perhaps looking for the folder I'd attempted to take from the travel
agency, Hal tried to pry the lid off one of the storage
crates. Meanwhile, I checked a luggage carrier to see
if something might have been left behind.

"Any luck?" I called to Hal. He'd gotten the lid off,
and was picking through what appeared to be cans of
soup and vegetables.

He shook his head and went for another crate.

I wasn't having much luck either. The luggage carrier was mostly empty except for a duffel bag filled

with packing material.

"Nothing here," Callie said, when I joined her at the desk.

The folders were full of receipts of various sorts—for things like maintenance equipment, oil deliveries, and plane repairs. I pulled a dark blue folder from the bottom of a stack, wondering if its color had any significance (the rest of the folders were plain manila). I closed my eyes and concentrated hard, running my fingers over the cover, but no images popped into my head.

I opened the folder. Inside was a map of Orion. Various points around town had been circled.

"What's that?" Callie asked.

"I'm not sure," I said, noting that the building on Rantoul Street—the pharmacy I'd visited with Amanda— was one of the circled points, as was the travel agency. "Check this out," I said to her, assuming that the other circled places were those once owned by the college.

A moment later, a loud banging sound cut through my core, stealing my breath. I turned to look. Hal had accidentally dropped one of the crate lids. I glanced toward the open hangar door, knowing that the security guard might have heard the noise.

Hal gestured to a large metal cabinet a few yards behind the guard's desk. We all ran to it and huddled in front of the doors as Hal fumbled with the combination lock.

At the same moment, it felt as if an electrical current

had shot through my veins. I stumbled back, feeling off-balance.

"What was that?" Callie whispered, making me wonder if she'd felt it, too. Smushed between the two of them, I touched the door hinge, suddenly able to picture a metal ladder and an underground room.

"The security guard's on his way back," Hal said. "He's only a minute away."

"How do you know?" I asked him.

Hal shook his head, seemingly at a loss for words. Meanwhile, Callie pushed her way in front of the lock. She squatted down and placed her ear up against it as she turned the dial, listening for the clicks to get the right combination.

I held my breath, suddenly noticing a bright red tag on the cabinet door. It read PROPERTY OF ORION COLLEGE OF PHARMACEUTICALS.

"He's about ten yards from the hangar," Hal said, referring to the guard.

Callie pulled at the lock, but it didn't open.

"What do we do?" I asked, huddling in even closer, praying that the guard wouldn't see us.

Callie took a deep breath and, in one quick motion, broke the lock apart, forcing it open by yanking at the dial. She tumbled back, landing on the concrete. Hal and I helped her up, each taking a hand. That same electrical current sensation moved down my spine.

"What's going on?" Hal asked.

We shook our heads, because none of us knew. The only thing for certain was that we didn't have time. "He's just about to round the corner," Hal said.

We yanked opened the cabinet, rushed inside, and shut the door behind us, only to discover that it wasn't a cabinet after all.

It was a door to an underground room. A wobbly metal ladder, just like the one I'd pictured moments ago, led us down twenty steps; I counted them to remain calm.

"What are you doing here?" a voice snapped before I'd even reached the bottom rung of the ladder.

I turned around, stunned by who we'd found.

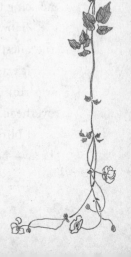

CHAPTER 23

Vice Principal Roger Thornhill was lying in a hospital bed staring back at us. There were monitors all around him, though it seemed like he was perfectly alert. Wearing a hospital gown, he looked weak, much thinner than I'd remembered him, even though it'd only been a couple of weeks.

"Mr. Thornhill, are you okay?" I took a step closer, noticing the bandage over his forehead.

"How did you find me?" he asked brusquely, ignoring the question. "Does anyone else know you're here?"

It was almost too loud to hear him. A clanging motor was running somewhere; the noise was coming from some overhead ductwork that ran along the ceiling.

I blinked a couple times, barely able to believe what I saw—he was harnessed to the bed: thick straps were across his legs, middle, and chest; and his hands and feet were shackled.

Hal moved to see if he could help free him—but Thornhill shook his head, making an effort to wrap his fingers around one of the straps, as if to pull it away from Hal.

"Don't you want to get out of here?" Hal asked, focused on Thornhill.

"I do," he said, "but it's best if they think they're in control."

"Best for whom?" I asked.

"For Amanda," he said, meeting my gaze. His eyes were red, sprinkled with broken blood vessels. "Dr. Joy and the Official need to believe that they're the ones in charge here."

"Aren't they?" Hal asked, nodding toward the straps.

I peered around the underground room. This was definitely a secret place. There were crude rock walls and a dirt floor. The smell of mildew was thick in the air. Unlike what we'd been told following Thornhill's absence, this was clearly not part of any sort of rehabilitation. This was incarceration. Why didn't he seem more relieved that we'd found him?

"We can get you out of here." I looked toward Callie, hoping she'd be able to help him, since she'd recently become our own personal locksmith. She stepped toward his bindings.

"Callista, no! Get *yourselves* out," he said. "It's better this way."

"Are you hurt?" Callie asked him.

"Don't worry about me. Worry about yourselves. You need to be careful with Dr. Joy and the Official. Staying out of their clutches is our only hope—our only chance for finding Amanda."

"But who exactly is this Dr. Joy?" I asked, wondering how Thornhill expected to help Amanda while being chained to a hospital bed. "What does he want?"

"Well, Amanda, of course," he said.

"Yes, but *why*?" I asked, desperate to know the truth.

"Because she was born; that's why. Don't you understand?" he asked, annoyance creeping into his voice, even as he struggled to be patient. "All of this stems from her birth—from the very fact that she was born. But listen to me. I can't explain now. Just get out of here."

I shook my head, still unclear. "Why?" I asked again.

"And—wait, who's the Official?" Hal interrupted.

A surprised look flashed across his pale, gaunt face. "Why don't you know any of this? I thought this was what you'd all be working on . . ." He trailed off, alarm in his voice.

I looked at Callie and Hal. Did he think Amanda had told us? Did she know any of these people?

"Joy's in some trouble, too," he continued. "It's the Official we really need to be afraid of."

"Who *is* the Official?" Callie asked.

He shook his head and gestured to what appeared to

be a heart monitor, perhaps concerned that it was bugged.

I approached the monitor, noticing the bright red tag right away. Like the cabinet we'd entered to get down here, the tag read PROPERTY OF ORION COLLEGE OF PHARMACEUTICALS, making me think back to my conversation with Amanda, when she'd hinted that the college was corrupt—or those who were once affiliated with it were—even though it was no longer open.

"We need some answers," Hal insisted, focusing on Thornhill. "We've been chasing clues since you got hurt, not knowing who to trust or what to believe. People tell us not to be together, but then those same people disappear. Amanda seems to be around every corner, but never in plain sight."

"Can't you give us any insight?" Callie pleaded.

"I can't get into anything now," Thornhill said, struggling to raise his voice above the sound of the motor. But then he looked uneasily back at the heart monitor, seemingly concerned his captors might hear him. "I'm sure you have a lot of what you already need. The four of you were able to find me, after all."

I exchanged confused looks with both Hal and Callie. "The four of us?"

"Sir," said Hal, "there's just us three."

Had his blow to the head been more severe than we originally thought? Four of us? An Official?

We looked back at him for some sort of explanation,

but he was gazing past us toward the ladder.

First we saw boots—black, worn, military-style, laced. Then ripped tights. A denim skirt and plaid shirt. Straight, shiny black hair. *Zoe Costas?* What was *she* doing here?

I felt my mouth drop open.

"*Huh?!*" Hal asked at the sight of her.

"Are you lost?" Callie asked.

I'd barely ever talked to Zoe Costas before. The extent of our interaction was limited to one time in French class when she'd asked to borrow a pen. Not that I think she talked to many other people more than that. Still, she seemed to slip effortlessly into any group—one day hanging out with the band geeks, the next day lunching with the most popular kids at school. Everyone knew who she was, but at the same time, nobody seemed to know her at all.

Zoe stared at us, her hazel eyes wide and impenetrable, but still she did not speak. She was shaking her head slightly, but I didn't know why. Was she disappointed? Was she surprised to learn that the situation was this dire?

"What is going on?" I demanded.

Still Zoe remained silent, eyes locked with Thornhill's.

Then I turned back to Thornhill, far less interested in Zoe Costas—for now, anyway—than I was about finding Amanda. "Tell us what we need to know," I demanded.

"How can we find Amanda?"

"You need to learn everything you can about a program called C-33," he said urgently. "It's the key to cracking this thing. Find out about Dr. Joy's original intent, then consider what would happen if that plan got hijacked."

"*What?*" I asked, trying to commit these details to memory.

"You'll find more answers in Washington, D.C.," he muttered, looking back at the heart monitor again. "Go there. And find Robin, Ariel's sister."

"Excuse me?" I asked, feeling my heart clench. The name *Ariel* was suddenly like a giant neon sign, flashing behind my eyes.

"He means Amanda." Zoe finally spoke. A small smile crossed her lips. "Ariel's her birth name."

"How do you know?" Hal asked, whipping his head toward her.

"I actually know more about Amanda than any of you." She pulled at a strand of her glossy dark hair, the underside of which was dyed cobalt blue.

I shook my head, completely at a loss. I mean, was it possible that Cryptic Zoe Costas could provide the missing piece in our whole jigsaw puzzle of an investigation?

"Care to elaborate?" Callie asked her. "Are you a part of this? Were you here all along, or did you follow us?"

I could see the inevitable shock of another Amanda betrayal in Hal's and Callie's eyes. I was not above feeling it myself, but being able to compartmentalize emotions comes in handy. "Wait," I said. "Mr. Thornhill, we've looked for you . . ."

"There isn't time," Thornhill snapped again. "I'm sorry. You really must go. They'll be back any minute."

"It's true—they will be back," Hal said.

Thornhill muttered something else about going upstairs and finding a key, but I could no longer even hear him now; his voice was barely audible over the motor.

"What?" I asked, taking a couple steps closer to hear him better.

And that's when I saw it.

Hanging around his neck.

An oval-shaped charm.

I immediately flashed back to Amanda's all-important box, thinking about the black-and-white photos we'd found—the one that had the heads cut out, possibly to fit inside a locket. It'd been a photo of a pregnant woman sitting beside a man (possibly the father), with a younger girl crouched in front.

I was just about to ask him if I could see the charm when a door slammed somewhere overhead. No time to ask him now.

"Go!" Thornhill insisted. Chained to a bed or not, the man was still intimidating.

"We can't just leave you here," Callie cried. She grabbed at the shackles around his middle.

"Get out of here. Now. I'm ordering you," he insisted. His eyes were full of anger. "Or else you'll end up here."

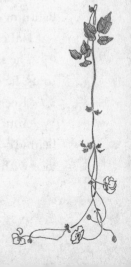

CHAPTER 24

Callie and Hal hurried up the ladder, while Zoe hesitated a bit, glancing back at Thornhill, as if she wanted to ask him something more. Was it something we didn't know? Something to explain what she was doing here? Or how she knew more about Amanda than we did?

I followed close behind on the ladder. We crammed ourselves back inside the closet-turned-doorway, and the lightning-bolt sensation soared through me again.

Hal edged the door open, as Zoe let out a tiny gasp.

The security guard had returned to his desk. His back to us, he pulled a bag of crackers from his drawer.

"Keep low," Hal whispered, signaling us to follow him. We crouched down, making our way slowly and carefully behind some storage crates. Once there, Callie covered her face with my scarf, all but stuffing it into her mouth to keep from crying out in sheer anxiety.

"We can't stay here," I mouthed to Hal.

The security guard leaned back in his seat, watching something on a portable TV as he sipped a can of soda.

I moved in the direction of the hangar door, knowing that in only a few feet I'd be in the guard's peripheral view.

Hal grabbed the back of my shirt to hold me in place. "Wait up," he whispered, reaching into my bag. He rifled around for a few seconds before taking out my vintage oyster-shell compact.

"What do you think you're doing?" I asked, keeping my voice low.

The next thing I knew, Hal was sitting up. His head above the crate, just beyond the guard's scope, he chucked the compact as hard as he could, clear across the hangar. It made a *clink* sound in a faraway corner by some storage boxes.

The guard shot up, grabbed his club, and went to check things out. Meanwhile, we hurried toward the exit. In doing so, my shoe made a skidding sound against the floor. Luckily the guard didn't seem to hear it.

Finally outside, I peered behind me, noticing that Callie had dropped the scarf.

"Just leave it," Hal said.

I looked back toward the scarf, in plain view, knowing that it would give us away immediately. And we needed all the time we could get to escape.

Keeping low, I scurried back inside the hangar. The

guard had his back to me, still searching for the source of the noise. I grabbed the scarf and ducked behind the set of stairs.

"Come on!" Hal whispered, waving me out.

I started to move toward him when the guard pivoted around.

And looked in my direction.

"Hello?" he called out, his hand clenched firmly over his billy club. It appeared he hadn't found my compact. "Is someone there?"

I remained crouched behind the stairs, relieved that he hadn't seen me. Sweat dripped from my brow. I wiped it on my sleeve and waited for his next move.

I scooted down even farther and held my breath.

A moment later, a side door opened toward the back of the hangar. A woman emerged. Wearing a fitted navy-blue suit with glossy blond hair slicked back in a high ponytail, she did not look familiar at first. But then she turned and I was able to see her face.

Her perfect doll's face.

It was Waverly Valentino.

"I found it, Barnaby," she shouted to the guard, holding up a folder. "Be sure to give this to him today." They exchanged a few words, their backs to me.

The perfect opportunity to scurry out.

I joined the others, noticing right away how the Jeep was parked by the tanker truck. "They're probably fueling up," I said, ducking behind an oil drum.

"They should be done about now," Hal said.

Without another word, we raced toward the fence, back through the gate; it was still open. Zoe tried to make things look intact to buy us time, threading the chain back through a link in the fence, and knotting the broken pieces together without having the lock slip off. But it was no use. The lock had obviously been tampered with—and they'd notice that right away.

"Um, guys?" Callie murmured, anxiety in her voice. "You need to see this." She held out her arm.

Where the deep bleeding gash had been, it was now completely healed. No mark, no blood. Gone.

Hal examined both her arms, making sure that we were looking at the right one. Both were perfect, completely unscathed.

I scanned my scarf; it was still damp and bloodstained from her injury.

"Weird, right?" Callie asked with a sickly smile. Her neck was covered in hives, which were working their way up her cheeks. We couldn't even react because a second later, a door slammed shut, making us all jump. The Jeep headed toward the gate.

Toward us.

We darted behind the bushes for our bikes. I tried to pull mine up from the ground, but the handlebars slipped from my grip and landed against Callie's back wheel.

"There isn't time," Hal insisted, waving from behind the bushes. We ducked under the foliage.

The Jeep came to a sudden halt about twenty yards away, just shy of the entrance gate. The guy with the bandana got out, fished in his pocket for a set of keys, and went to open the lock.

Meanwhile, my heart pounded and my stomach lurched, especially since my entire left side was completely exposed, sticking out from the bushes. I peeked out at the gate. The driver was inspecting the broken chain. But instead of responding with alarm, he merely unthreaded both the chain and the padlock from the gate's loop, threw them in the Jeep, and drove away, back toward the hangar.

I grappled for my bike again. Finally, I untangled it. Callie and Hal got hold of their bikes, and it turned out Zoe had one, too. Had she followed us here?

I stuffed the scarf inside my bag. We were just about to ride away, when a loud siren blared angrily from the hangar, as if someone had just escaped from prison.

"What the hell is that?" Hal asked, covering his ears.

Zoe gestured to the overhead lights flashing from the hangar's roof. There was no question: they knew we'd broken in.

And now they were coming after us.

CHAPTER 25

We sped away, back down the dirt road, cutting across a field with a well-worn trail, and then over a gravel-lined path. Aside from the blare of the siren, getting fainter with each pedal, there was only the sound of breathing as we struggled to get away.

After several minutes en route, a loud popping sound came from somewhere behind me. I looked over my shoulder. Zoe was floundering on her bike. Her wheels were wavering from side to side over the gravel.

"What's going on?" I asked her.

She shook her head, trailing behind us at least three yards. "Not sure. I can't keep up."

But there was no way that we could stop for a break. They would be in close pursuit. We kept pedaling.

"And why the sirens?" Hal panted. "I can't imagine

they'd want to attract attention. I mean, call me crazy, but if I had someone chained up in my basement, I'd want to keep it on the down low."

"Maybe attention doesn't matter to them. Maybe the police are on their side," I said through my teeth, thinking about Chief Bragg and Officer Marciano.

"Are we even close to town?" Callie asked, barely winded as she pedaled.

Hal shook his head, completely at a loss. This detour seemed to be leading us farther away from anything even remotely familiar.

About a mile later, Zoe announced that she was having trouble with her gears. We finally stopped to inspect her bike and discovered the source of the popping noise.

Her tire was flat. A nail had punctured the rubber.

"You can ride on my handlebars," Callie told her.

"Seriously?" Hal stifled a laugh.

"Are *you* serious?" I asked him, surprised that he was even questioning it. "Because you're obviously forgetting Super Callie, who got us through the chained gate and into that basement, opening two locks with her bare hands."

Callie grinned at me. "How about we take a break for a minute?" She wiped the sweat off her brow with the hem of her baby-doll dress, and then pointed to what appeared to be an abandoned barn up ahead. There were no cars around it, the gardens were all overgrown, and the path leading up to it was covered with tall grass and sprawling brush.

"There's no sense riding farther toward nothingness,"

Zoe agreed, pulling a map from her back pocket.

"Plus, I doubt those guys will find us now," Callie added.

"Okay," Hal said, still a bit reluctant. "But only for a few minutes. I want to get back soon. I have a feeling it gets really dark out here with no streetlights."

We walked our bikes around to the front of the barn. It had definitely been abandoned. A splattering of graffiti adorned the kicked-in double doors, including a tag that read *Voodoo Lives*.

Hal pointed to a busted padlock, still hanging from the door latch. "Are you sure you haven't been here before?" he asked Callie.

"Funny." She rolled her eyes and pushed the door all the way open.

We followed, wheeling our bikes into the barn.

It had surely attracted a party crowd. Beer bottles and snack bags were strewn all over the floor, and the interior walls had been tagged as well. The words *Pig*, *Tarot Tales*, and *Voodoo Dies* (clever corollary of *Voodoo Lives*) were painted all over the crude barn walls.

"*Tarot*," Callie whispered, referring to the lobster card that Bea got at the hospital.

"Coincidence?" Hal asked.

"I honestly don't know anymore." I plunked down on one of the many bales of hay, put my head between my knees, and tried to breathe through the tunneling sensation inside my chest. Finally, after several moments, when

I was able to regain my composure, I sat back up and narrowed my eyes at Zoe. Framed in the barn's doorway, she had none of her usual armor from school—her camera or her saxophone—yet she looked completely guarded. "So, how did you get here again?" I asked her.

"On Callie's handlebars, remember?" she said evenly. "That was me on the bike with the blown-out tire."

"You know what she means." Hal was very quiet, almost eerily so. "I think now would be a good enough time to explain yourself."

"According to *you* it's a good enough time," she said, still lingering by the entrance doors. "But from where I'm standing, not so much."

"Well, I'm with them," Callie said. "And we need an explanation."

Zoe shook her head and folded her arms in front. "Believe me. It's not the time."

"Then when?" Hal snapped, taking a seat beside me. "I mean, who do you even think you are?"

"Did you follow us from school? Or were you already at the hangar when we arrived?" I continued, remembering when Hal thought he'd heard something outside the gate.

"Look," Zoe said, "I'll know when the time is right. That's all I can say. I'm sorry to shock you guys. But if you'd been through what I have, you'd be cautious, too."

"What's that supposed to mean?" Callie asked. "What have you been through?"

"Not *now*," she said again, her eyes almost boring into Callie's. For a second, she looked so sad, I almost felt bad pushing her.

Then, she was almost apologetic. "I can't."

I suddenly stopped caring about what she was doing here. It was like she managed to make herself invisible, to fade a little. Two seconds ago, figuring out what she was doing had been priority number one. But now, I felt my questions slipping away. It was so strange. Zoe was not an immediate danger, but the guys chasing us were—and we needed to regroup before they found us.

"Can someone please just tell me what the hell is going on here?" Callie asked, rubbing her temples in frustration. Later, she told me she experienced the same sudden shift in priorities—her own "these are not the droids you are looking for" moment.

"Or what just happened?" I added.

"Thornhill will probably be in even more danger now. They'll definitely know we went down there and saw him. I mean, we broke that lock, too."

"As if I couldn't feel worse." Callie sighed, pacing back and forth over a pile of candy wrappers. "They probably won't even keep him there now. They'll assume we'll go to the authorities and blow the whistle about his where-abouts."

"If only we could trust the 'authorities,'" Hal said.

"And I saw Waverly," I told them.

187

"At the hangar?" Callie's eyes grew wide.

I nodded and looked at Zoe, a bit self-conscious to be revealing information in front of her. "When I went back to get the scarf, Waverly came in through a side door to talk to the guard."

"So, she's definitely one of them." Hal grabbed a water bottle from his bag and drank half of it. "Like there was any doubt, but at least now we know for sure."

"There's something else, too," I ventured, unable to get the image out of my mind. "Did anyone else happen to notice the necklace that Thornhill was wearing?"

Both Callie and Hal shook their heads. Callie said, "I was too busy trying to calculate how to disengage him from all those machines so that any alarm would only be triggered once . . . not to mention the angle to best get him up the ladder, tied to his stretcher."

Zoe was back to playing with her hair, managing to hide her face.

"It was oval-shaped and tarnished," I told them. "I think it might've been a locket."

"On a guy?" Callie asked.

"Plenty of men wear lockets, especially men in the service," I explained. "They wear them because they're away from their families, and they can put photos inside . . . to keep their loved ones close to their heart."

"Right," Callie agreed. "But last I checked, Thornhill wasn't *in* the service."

"No, but maybe he's separated from his family," Hal mused.

"Well, he *is* being kept captive." Callie tapped her chin in thought.

"My point is that the photo we found in Amanda's box . . . the one with the heads cut out—"

"Whoa," Hal said, interrupting me. "You don't think those heads are in Thornhill's alleged locket?"

"It's something to consider," I said, nodding. "Maybe Thornhill's more connected to Amanda's disappearance than we thought."

"Which would explain how he knew she had an older sister," Callie said. "As well as her real name."

"He was her vice principal with access to her records," I reminded Callie. "He could've known just by looking at her file." I paused a moment. "Of course, *we* couldn't find them. Plus any file of Amanda's would probably be false, given all the stories she told us. But still, somehow, he does seem to know about her."

"Wait, you don't think Thornhill will tell those guards where to find us, do you?" Hal asked.

I shook my head, remembering how adamant he'd been about letting those guys think that they were in charge. I shot him a withering look. "He'll try to play dumb, like he didn't know who we were, and say that he never even spoke to us."

"Yes, but what if they have it all on tape?" Hal asked.

"Thornhill won't rat us out," Zoe said. The sound of her voice was such a shock, it took me a second to understand what she just said. Whatever feeling I'd had before, that mysterious forgetting about Zoe's presence? That was gone now, the spell broken.

"How do *you* know?" Callie asked.

"Because I know him—obviously a lot better than any of you. He is on our side."

"Just like you know Amanda?" I scoffed a bit. "And that Amanda's name is supposedly Ariel?"

"Possibly," Zoe said, completely inscrutable.

"Care to explain?" Hal asked her.

Zoe hiked up her sleeves, revealing a chunky beaded bracelet that I could've sworn I'd seen on Amanda. When she saw that I'd noticed, she rolled her sleeves back down.

"*Well?*" Callie asked, her arms folded, trying to appear intimidating despite the ballet flats and baby-doll dress.

"Thornhill was friends with my parents in another life." Zoe shrugged. "When I was younger, like three or four, he'd come to our house sometimes, bring little presents to me and my sisters, and then he and my parents would go out on the back porch while we played with our new trinkets. His name was not Thornhill then. And he'd moved by the time I was in first grade. Seriously, it was really no big deal."

"News flash, but Thornhill having another life *is* a big deal," I told her.

"Plus, if it was *really* no big deal," Hal continued, "then what are you even doing here?"

"I've actually been following you for the past couple weeks." She shrugged.

"What?" I asked, feeling my stomach twist, but was somehow not completely surprised. We often had the sense we were being followed—why not Zoe?

"It's true." She was again deadpan, as if trailing kids around in high school was as normal as varsity cheerleading tryouts.

"But why?" Callie asked, shocked.

"Because I'm looking for Amanda, too."

"Yes, but *why* are you looking for her?" I asked, my voice cold and inquisitorial.

"Why are *you*?" Zoe volleyed back.

"Amanda is our friend," I said, an edge to my voice.

Zoe toyed with the beaded bracelet, not even trying to hide it now. "Well, she's my friend, too."

I shook my head, reminded once again of how little I knew about Amanda, and how many secrets—and secret friends—she obviously had.

"How do we know that?" Callie asked.

"What do you want me to say?" Zoe shrugged. "Amanda and I spent a lot of time together before she disappeared. You know she was a talented jazz pianist, right? We were a duo—we played at Arcadia."

"Um, *what*?" Callie's lips parted in surprise.

"Seriously, you should see her play," Zoe said.

"Amanda didn't perform music—she liked it, but

never said she could play," Hal argued.

"Well, you obviously don't know her as well as you think you do," Zoe retorted.

A direct hit. I could see the pain in Hal's eyes. He stood up from his hay bale, clearly jealous.

"Well, I guess that sort of makes sense," Callie said, pondering aloud. "That Amanda was into music, I mean. She was pretty much into—and good at—just about everything cultural, literary, and artistic."

"So, what do you know about her family?" I asked Zoe, curious to hear what kind of story Amanda had given her, in comparison to the various tales she'd told us.

"I mentioned I knew her *sister*," she corrected me. "Amanda and I lived in the same town for a while— Pinkerton—until she, her mother, and Robin moved away one day. Just like that. With absolutely no warning whatsoever. No one had any idea that they'd even been thinking about it. I just rode by on my bike one day, and saw the FOR RENT sign."

"Oh," I said, completely startled that we were finally getting the truth, and that it was so different from what the three of us had been told. "So you knew Amanda *pre*-Orion."

"Oh, right," Callie said.

Hal took a deep breath, taken aback by the news as well. "And where was Amanda's father?" he asked.

"Dead was what they said," Zoe answered. "But sometimes Amanda would say he was traveling, or otherwise out of the picture. I never met him, they didn't really like to talk about him, and I'm not even sure that Amanda knew who he was. Anyway, Amanda's sister, Robin, was older, but she was really great, always taking us places . . . to the park, to get ice cream, or for bike rides."

"And Amanda's mother?" I asked.

"She was great, too—super creative and uber-energetic—but she was always busy doing other things, so I barely ever saw her. It's really sad that she died in that car accident."

"Thornhill said Robin's in Washington, D.C.," I said. "Do you know why?"

"And is Amanda with her?" Callie asked.

"Enough questions," Zoe said. "Now it's my turn."

"You don't make the rules," Hal objected.

"Oh, no?" Her eyebrow perked up. "Keep in mind that I wasn't really planning to join your search. I was doing just fine on my own."

"So, why did you?" Callie asked.

"I already told you; it's my turn for questions. May I?" Zoe moved to snag Hal's water bottle, he passed it, and she took a giant sip and then wiped her mouth on her sleeve. "Where are you now in the search?"

"We have a website that explains it all," Hal said. "Look it up: theamandaproject.com."

Zoe rolled her eyes. "I know there's more. You wouldn't put everything on the site where anyone could see it."

"Well, don't you think that if Amanda had wanted

you to know the more privileged clues, she'd have given them to you herself?" Hal asked.

"Who says she hasn't?" Zoe arched an eyebrow.

"Me," Hal said. "Otherwise you wouldn't be here."

"Maybe Amanda doesn't trust you as much as you'd like to think she does," I chimed in.

"Funny"—Zoe paused for another sip—"that's exactly what Amanda said you'd say."

"Excuse me?" I felt my eyes narrow.

"There's a lot about me that you don't know," she said.

Her statement couldn't have been truer: Zoe always seemed to be in the background of everything, almost invisible and yet everywhere at the same time. "Like what?" I asked, eager for an explanation.

"Well, for starters," she began, "*unlike* all of you, I didn't agree to be Amanda's guide . . . at least not right away."

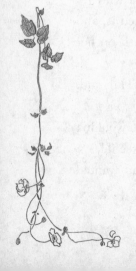

CHAPTER 26

"How many guides does one person actually need?" Callie squawked, holding her head in her hands.

We were all sitting in a circle of hay bales now, sharing lunch leftovers—Cheez-Its, gummy worms, and my mother's homemade granola.

"Seriously, I barely even feel like I know her now," Callie continued.

Hal, too, still seemed upset. His arms were folded, and he was much quieter than usual.

I, on the other hand, was over any notion of *upset*. What I wanted was answers. I turned to Zoe, interrupting her from stuffing an obscenely realistic-looking gummy worm into her mouth. "Why didn't you agree to be Amanda's guide right away?"

"Because of what I've seen," she said.

"Care to elaborate?" I asked.

She shook her head. "If you knew what I know, you might not be so eager to dish all the details either."

"Did Amanda want you to do something that made you uncomfortable?" Callie asked.

"Let's just say that I *saw* something that made me uncomfortable. And what I lived through was even worse."

I wanted to ask her more, but I could see she was getting emotional—her face was blotchy and her hands kept fidgeting.

"Amanda's world can seem pretty exciting at times," she continued, "but it can also be downright terrifying."

We exchanged looks—and silently agreed not to press her right away.

"So, how about catching me up to speed," Zoe suggested. "Tell me what I need to know about your search so far."

"If you've been following us, then you should know for yourself," Hal said.

I took a deep breath, holding myself back from launching a gummy worm at his head. His obvious pride was clearly getting in the way of hearing Zoe out.

"We owe it to Amanda to give Zoe a chance," I told him.

"Why?" he asked.

"Because I'm a guide just like you," Zoe said, giving a

nervous tug to her cobalt-blue hair.

"Prove it," he said.

Zoe looked back and forth between him and Callie, as if choosing her words carefully. "I was there that night . . . on Crab Apple Hill," she said finally. "And I overheard everything."

It had been a couple of weeks since what had happened on Crab Apple Hill. A couple of weeks since we had all received cryptic messages from Amanda, ordering us to meet at the very top. Only once there, contrary to what Amanda had promised us, she'd never even come. We ended up alone, and yet together at the same time.

Callie sat up straight on her bale, and the color drained from her face. That night on Crab Apple Hill was the night when she'd told us about Beatrice Rossiter's accident, and how she'd helped Heidi to cover it up by acting as an alibi.

Obviously Zoe had heard the confession, too.

The weird thing was that I wasn't too surprised that Zoe had been there that night. I remembered hiking up to the top, hearing a female voice call out Amanda's name a couple times, and thinking how the voice sounded way deeper than Callie's. I also remembered hearing footsteps that couldn't be accounted for, and wondering if they might've belonged to Amanda. Now I knew it had been Zoe.

"It was really brave of you to open up like that," Zoe

said, turning toward Callie, "and to figure out how to make it right."

"Yeah, well . . . ," Callie said, and looked away, pleased for the praise but still her eyes filled with tears.

I handed her a tissue from my bag, and Hal offered her some water.

"So, if you're really a guide"—Hal turned to Zoe— "then you must have a totem, too."

"According to Amanda, everyone has a totem." She smiled.

I smiled, too. Because it was true. Amanda has this thing about totems—basically that we all have animal spirit guides that look after and protect us. My totem was the night owl, symbolic of wisdom and intuition, both of which stem from burying myself in books, doing what I believe to be just, and observing others' actions from afar.

"Amanda stenciled my totem on my locker that night, just like she did with all of yours," Zoe continued. "A chameleon."

"Ever changing," I said, thinking how it made complete sense.

"But Thornhill must not have seen your totem," Hal said, referring to how Thornhill had called the three of us into his office to accuse us of graffitiing his car and explain the tagging on our lockers.

"Yes, but then why did he seem to know that we belonged together?" I asked, remembering how, in the hangar basement, he'd referred to the *four* of us.

"Maybe Amanda told him?" Hal shrugged.

"It didn't sound like he'd even *seen* Amanda," Callie argued.

Zoe looked clueless as well. Between bites of gummy-worm-and-Cheez-It sandwiches, she went on to explain how, on the day that our lockers were tagged, she'd gotten to school extra early to finish up some pieces for the school newspaper, where she was in charge of the final layout as the photography editor. En route to the journalism room, she'd spotted the totem right away. "I scrubbed it off before Thornhill saw," she explained. "Some pretty heavy stuff had just gone down, and I didn't want anyone to see it—to know that I'd been connected with Amanda in any way."

"Heavy stuff?" Callie asked.

"Amanda stuff," she said, remaining as mysterious as Amanda herself. "Amanda had wanted me to be a part of your group—to help you guys search for her. But, after everything that'd happened, shadowing your investigation was as close as I was willing to get. Until this." Zoe reached into her bag again and pulled out a card. On the front was a print from Henri Matisse's *Jazz* series.

I'd recognize it anywhere. In the sixth grade, Ms. MacKenzie, our art teacher, had us do a whole unit on Matisse's career. The *Jazz* series was particularly interesting, because unlike Matisse's other work, it'd been made up of colorful paper cutouts assembled on gouache-painted paper. This particular print was from the front cover of his *Jazz* book, a compilation of more of his work done in the same style.

"It was her way of trying to rope me in again," Zoe explained, pointing out the chameleon totem inked in the corner of the card. "Amanda knows how passionate I am about jazz. Anyway, this one's my copy . . . and these are yours." She reached into her bag a final time, and pulled out three more *Jazz* cards. "When I got to the airstrip, I found these clipped to the spokes of your bike wheels. She did the same with my card; only I got mine yesterday, when I had my bike parked behind the library."

"So, she was here?" Callie asked. "At the airstrip, while we were inside the hangar?"

"Looks like it." I sighed. "And she's still playing games."

"Not games," Hal said, coming to Amanda's defense. "There's a reason she can't show herself, remember?"

"Yes, but it's pretty easy to forget that while trying to outrun armed guards in the middle of nowhere and dump-the-body-land, where the only adult who seems to believe you is literally tied up," I snapped at him.

"Amanda comes so close," Callie said, thinking aloud, "giving herself ample time to dig up clue cards and pin them to our bikes. So, why not come just a little bit closer and actually talk to us—give us a *real* clue as to what's going on?"

"Because she can't," Zoe stated simply. Instead she handed us our *Jazz* cards.

As with Zoe's, Amanda had inked our individual totems in the corners.

"The little bear is mine," Callie said, taking her card.

"And I'll take the cougar," Hal said.

My card was on the bottom. The night owl looked almost as if it were grinning at me—as if this *were* indeed one big game.

A game that couldn't be won.

I ran my fingers over the card, wondering if I'd envision anything. As I did, my finger brushed across something on the back side. "What's this?" I asked, flipping the card over.

There was a poem on the back. Apparently Amanda had pasted it to my card.

"What is it?" Hal asked.

"'The Road Less Traveled,'" I whispered, "by Robert Frost." I looked at the back of their *Jazz* cards, but they were all blank.

And so this message was just for me.

"What's 'The Road Less Traveled' have to do with anything?" Callie asked.

I bit my lip, knowing all too well what the message meant. The memory was still vivid, like it had happened only yesterday.

With my parents' permission, Amanda and I took a trip into the city to see a special exhibit of Vincent Van Gogh's work. Like much of my time with Amanda, the whole experience was completely surreal. Several of the paintings had come from the Van Gogh Museum in Amsterdam, as well as the Metropolitan Museum of Art in New York and the Getty Center in California.

And now they were right in front of us: *Starry Night, Starry Night over the Rhone, Irises,* and *The Night Café* . . .

We were halfway through Van Gogh's *Sunflower* series, when Amanda grabbed my arm and ushered me into another room entirely. "Look at this one," she said, pointing to an Impressionist piece. The title was *The Road Less Traveled,* by an anonymous artist.

"Do you think it's a tribute to the poem?" I asked.

"Could be." She gave me a mysterious smile. "Or it could also be a sign that you need to branch out a bit . . . explore some new and uncharted territory."

"What do you mean?" I asked.

"I mean that all work and no play makes Jack a dull boy," she said, answering with a proverb. "Or in this case, it makes Jill a dull girl." She smiled, softening the blow.

I opened my mouth, unsure of how to respond and disappointed that she saw me that way. Because ever since Amanda Valentino had come into my life, I felt like I'd been "playing" more than ever.

"Remember to be open to that which crosses your path," she continued when I didn't answer.

"Where is all of this coming from?" I asked her.

"It's coming from me: Amanda Valentino." She smiled

wider. "Because Amanda thinks it would be absolutely tragic if her good friend Nia Antonia Rivera were to miss out on something great because she is so wrapped up in the routine of work."

"I'm not missing out on anything," I retorted, irritated that she would think so. "There's much more to my life than work."

"Of course there is," she said. "But, still, you have to admit, you're not the most trusting individual. And you've meandered down this path of distrust and standoffishness for far too long. It's time to take another road."

I looked away—toward the road-less-traveled painting—noticing the path that forked in two directions.

Amanda slipped her arm around my shoulder and gave me a squeeze. "Not everyone who crosses your path is going to hurt you, you know. There are some really remarkable people out there, and you deserve to meet them. And they, in turn, deserve to get close enough to know what a remarkable person you are as well—just as I do."

"These cards are proof that Amanda wants us to work together," Zoe asserted, plucking me out of my daydream. She muttered something else about visiting a Matisse exhibit, but I was barely even focusing on her words.

"Nia?" Callie asked, reaching out to touch my forearm.

Instead of answering, I looked back down at the Robert Frost poem, and that's when I noticed.

The postage stamp just beneath it.

On it was a picture of a 1974 Alfa Romeo. The words "A Classic: Built to Face the Road Head On" were printed on its racetrack.

I felt a smile cross my lips, wondering how Amanda could possibly have known. Had she spotted me eyeballing him in the parking lot earlier? Had she seen him drop by Hal's place the other night? Maybe she'd noticed him reading *Letters to a Young Poet* somewhere and suspected we'd have a lot in common.

"Nia!" Callie bellowed into my ear.

I opened my mouth, trying to find the words. I was so used to always having the most perfect response in every situation. But, as Amanda had pointed out, this was definitely new territory.

Tired of waiting for me, Hal grabbed my *Jazz* card and flipped it over to see the stamp. "This is just like West's car," he said.

"'A classic,'" Callie read over his shoulder, "'built to face the road head on.'"

"Do you know what it means?" Zoe asked.

"It probably just means that Amanda likes classic cars." He shrugged.

"A classic car that's the same exact make and model as West Kincaid's?" Callie asked. "With the same exact bronze color? And the same exact year?"

"Did Amanda even know West?" I finally found my voice.

Hal shook his head. "Not that I know of."

"Well, personally, I think this is *more* than a coincidence," Callie said.

"So then the question becomes: What does West have to do with our search?" Zoe asked.

"Maybe nothing." Callie smiled. "Maybe the question we should really be asking is: What does West Kincaid have to do with Nia? Did anyone else notice how West could barely keep his eyes off Nia the other night? It was like she'd lost her glass slipper and he had it stashed inside his pocket."

"It was actually a book on poetry," I said, correcting her.

"Even better." She brightened up even more. "A match made in Literary Heaven."

"Okay, I'll play. But how would Amanda have known that this West character was all foaming-at-the-mouth for Nia? And, no offense, why would we care?" Zoe asked.

"Honestly, I'm over questioning what Amanda knows," Callie said, "because she seems to be just about *everywhere*, and knows just about *everything*."

"At least everything pertaining to us." I took a deep breath, picturing myself walking down a less-traveled road, and knowing that Amanda was right. There were definitely amazing people in this world. People that I could trust.

Like the people in this room.

"May I?" Zoe asked, turning to Hal. Before he could answer, she snatched the card out of his grip and looked closely at the stamp. "Okay, let's take a look at his car at our first opportunity."

"Good point," Hal said. "And can we stop talking about West now? It's kind of freaking me out."

I couldn't have agreed more. My stomach still rumbled with hunger, and I was in desperate need of brain fuel. Then I remembered that my mother had packed me some afterschool snacks. I'd told her that Hal, Callie, and I were going to the Villa after school for a Humphrey Bogart movie marathon.

I opened her bag of treats, surprised to find that she'd given me four colossal, no-way-you-could-eat-more-than-just-one, double-fudge, chipotle-infused brownies, as well as four napkins and four boxes of juice. Obviously enough for each of us, including Zoe.

A lucky coincidence, or something more?

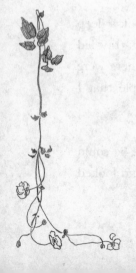

CHAPTER 27

We wound up in the barn for a little while longer, eating my mom's brownies and deciding our next steps. Zoe became the necessary piece in our jigsaw puzzle of an investigation, filling us in on what she knew about Amanda and her family—basically that Amanda, her sister, Robin, and her mother traveled around a lot, inexplicably moving from place to place.

"When Amanda first got to Orion," Zoe told us, "she said that she was staying with a friend of her mother's."

"Do you know the friend's name?" Hal asked.

Zoe shook her head. "Course not. Amanda was always so secretive about everything. Not only did she change mailing addresses constantly, but she also changed her name a bunch of times. She shed it like an outgrown skin. When we lived in Pinkerton, she went by Arabella."

"Excuse me?" Hal asked.

"It's true," Zoe said, warming to her role as sage. There was a knowing smile across her pale chapped lips.

"Holy aliases, Batman," Callie said. "That's so seriously weird. I'm still adjusting to Ariel."

"I know, and speaking of . . . remember the gift she left me—the first-edition copy of Sylvia Plath's *Ariel*? Some part of her wanted us to know that she changed her name."

"Let's also not forget about the hospital bracelet in Amanda's box," Hal continued, proceeding to tell Zoe about the maternity ward bracelet/ring. "Except the name on the bracelet was Ariel Feckerol."

"Feckerol, Valentino, Beckendorf . . . ," Callie sighed. "Which one's legit?"

"Good question," I said. "And here's another one: If that was indeed Amanda's baby bracelet, then what was Thornhill doing wearing it in the photo I found under the vase on my mother's desk?"

"Hold up," Zoe said, in desperate need of more filling in.

And so while Hal and Callie did just that, I got up from our circle of bales and paced the floor, scarfing down the remainder of my brownie. "Call me crazy," I began, unable to get the question out of my mind. "But has anyone considered the fact that Thornhill is related to Amanda in some way?"

"Like an uncle or a cousin?" Hal asked.

"Or her father," I said, releasing a ten-pound pause in the conversation.

"Okay, first of all, *what the . . . ?*" Callie said. "And, second of all, *no*. I mean, it can't be, right?"

"Well, it would certainly explain his involvement in all this," I said. "Not to mention why he's willing to remain locked up in a hangar basement because he thinks it will help keep Amanda safe."

"It does sort of make sense," Hal admitted.

Zoe couldn't argue either, making me wonder if she had known it all along.

"But if Thornhill is Amanda's father, then why is he keeping it a secret?" Callie asked.

"Think about it," Zoe said. "I mean, if it *is* true, then his wife—Amanda's mother—is dead. She was killed. Do you really believe that was an accident, especially considering that he, himself, was attacked, and that Amanda's in hiding? He might have no other choice *but* to keep secrets."

"Do you think Amanda knows he's her father?" I asked, assuming that it *was* indeed true.

"I'd tend to doubt it," Hal said. "I mean, the items in her box seemed so fragmented . . . so searching—the maternity bracelet, the photo with the heads cut out. I'll bet she doesn't know. Or didn't know when she collected all those scraps."

"So, then, what do these people want with this family?"

I asked, thinking out loud.

We sat in silence for several more moments, going over each question while still trying to flesh the theory out.

"I wonder why Thornhill no longer has the hospital bracelet," Hal ventured finally. "I mean, how did it end up in Amanda's box?"

"Who knows," Callie said. "But the fact that he once wore it certainly explains why the ring was so big. Like I said, it was definitely big enough for a man's finger."

"And like *he* said," Zoe continued, "all of this search business basically stems from Amanda's birth—from the fact that she was ever born."

"Well, and since we're on the topic of curious items stored in Amanda's all-important box," Hal began, "why would someone hold on to a photo that has the heads cut out of it? I mean, wouldn't you normally just throw those scraps away?"

"Not if you're hoping to fit them together with the missing photo-heads when you find them," Zoe said. "That's what I'd do, especially if I wanted to be sure who my father was. Perhaps that's the missing clue."

"Hang on a second," Callie said, holding the apparent ache in her head. "This is going way too fast. I mean, Thornhill? Amanda's father? Just picture the two of them together. Thornhill hates Amanda. All they do is fight."

Zoe cocked her head. "And you never fight with your dad? What was the birth date on the bracelet?"

"February thirteenth," I said, remembering how it was

just one day shy of Valentine's Day.

"Okay, but Amanda told me she was born on New Year's Eve," Callie said.

"No she wasn't," Hal argued. "Her birthday's in the summer. I know, because she said she wanted to have a party on the beach this year—just a small group thing with a bonfire and some food . . . She even mentioned there'd be a full moon."

"Here's a news flash: Those were all red herrings," Zoe said. "Because she and I just celebrated her birthday. It was last month. We went to Café Carla's and had red velvet cupcakes and mocha lattes with extra whipped cream."

I racked my brain, trying to remember if Amanda and I had ever even talked about her birthday, but aside from a conversation about astrology, and the fact that she was a Capricorn—which is a December/January astro-logical sign—I honestly couldn't recall.

"This is all so messed up," Callie said, rubbing at her temples.

"But not as messed up as your arm," Hal said, nod-ding toward it.

Callie slid her fingers over the now-invisible gash. I pulled the scarf from my bag. Her bloodstains were as clear as day. And yet her wound was completely gone.

"What's up with that?" Hal asked.

"And what's up with all the C-33 program stuff?" I asked, realizing we had yet to discuss it. "What did

Thornhill mean by Dr. Joy's 'original intent'?" I looked to Zoe to see if she might know; but if she did, she didn't let on.

"Well, obviously he was referring to the list of names with all the coding," Hal said.

"Yes, but what *is* the program?" I asked.

"I'm guessing it was something started by Dr. Joy," Hal said. "And the Official, whoever he or she is, intercepted it."

"It might also have something to do with the former Orion College of Pharmaceuticals . . . or at least what's happening at some of those buildings." I told them about the "Property-Of" tags I'd spotted at the hangar, after which I caught Zoe up on all the serpent-and-bowl-with-the-onyx-eye business.

"So, let me get this straight," Zoe began, "Amanda warned you that someone who was once affiliated with the college—some scientist or something—might be behind some of this C-33-Amanda-gone-missing stuff?"

"Maybe," I said, remembering that when Amanda and I had visited the pharmacy on Rantoul Street, the woman who'd answered the door was wearing a lab coat that said ORION COLLEGE OF PHARMACEUTICALS. "Why else would the hangar have some of the college's property?"

"And why else would the C-33 people only use those campus buildings?" Hal asked. "They must own all of them. And like Amanda said, they must use the onyx eye as a marker for colleagues to find them."

"And then they rent out the various buildings when they are finished with them," Callie continued. "So that they're always one step ahead."

"Yes, but the hangar doesn't belong to the college," Zoe said, fidgeting slightly on her bale of hay. "There was no serpent-and-bowl marker outside it."

"Right, but it's also located someplace remote," I told her. "Not in the middle of a bustling town."

"Bottom line: We definitely need to go to Washington, D.C.," Hal said. "We need to find out who this Official is, and why Dr. Joy started the C-33 program."

"We don't even know who Dr. Joy is," Callie said. "I mean, not really."

It's true—we didn't. I felt like all we had were bits and pieces of fragmented information that, when all put together, didn't really amount to much. "Okay, one last question before my mind short-circuits: What happened in the closet-turned-doorway . . . the one that led down to the hangar basement?" I asked, referring to the surge of energy when we all came together.

No one answered. But no one denied that *something* took place. They just sat there, staring at me, without admitting what they'd obviously experienced.

"Let's try it again," I told them.

I moved to stand in the center of the bales and gestured for them to join me. Hal hesitated at first, but then he got up and took my hand. Callie stood up and took his.

"I don't know." Zoe sat firmly in place.

"Come on," I said, extending my hand to hers. "You're a guide, too, after all."

After a long look, Zoe finally got up and clasped my hand, closing the circle by taking Callie's hand, too.

It was just as I'd expected. Electricity coursed through my veins and ran over my skin. I looked at Hal. His eyes were closed and his lips pressed together, as if he were someplace else entirely. As if he clearly felt it, too.

Zoe took a step back to break the circle.

Callie let out a breath, as if she'd been holding it the entire time. "What *was* that?" she asked.

I shook my head, because I honestly didn't know. But still I could feel it—a tingling sensation over my skin. It crept up my spine and swam down my limbs.

"Let's do it again," Zoe said.

I nodded and took her hand. Callie and Hal followed suit, until we were one solid ring.

The feeling was even more intense this time—I almost had to pull away. My heart beat fast and my head started spinning.

"We have to go," Hal announced suddenly, dropping hands. "Those guys are close. I can feel it. They're as far as the gravel path, at least a mile or two back, in the golf cart. One of them has a gun."

"The guys from the hangar?" I asked.

He nodded and looked away, seemingly freaked by

what he'd just experienced—by what he was able to sense so clearly.

"*How* can you feel it?" Callie asked.

He collected his bag and moved toward the door. "I just know, okay?" We all started grabbing our stuff and followed.

"Like what happened in the hangar basement," I asked. "When you *just knew* those guys would be returning soon."

"I may be stating the obvious—but I'm with this guy. Let's leave before the gun gets here," Zoe said.

"Flight seems like a very good option right now," Callie agreed. "But, um, can we talk about *all* of this later? I mean the vision and the powers . . ."

"When there is time." I looked toward the door, still open a crack, just to be safe. It was getting dark. We still had a long ride home. And we obviously needed to hurry if we wanted to get out of there before they found us.

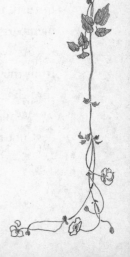

CHAPTER 28

We ended up ditching Zoe's tire-blown bicycle inside the barn. There was no time to walk it home, with those guys hot on our trail.

Darkness was quickly approaching. It was five o'clock and overcast outside, and the twilight was bringing a descending mist, which didn't give us a lot of daylight left. As if scary men with guns were not enough reason to rush, the talent show started at seven, and Hal's band members were counting on him to play.

As we pedaled down a long dirt path heading away from the barn, I kept glancing over my shoulder, making sure that no one was following us.

While Zoe balanced on Callie's handlebars, doing her best not to topple off, she tried to make sense of her map as it flapped and bounced. "Ah, I see exactly where we are," she said, turning the map in an unlikely direction to see if that would make a difference.

Meanwhile, I tried to keep myself calm by going over some of the clues in my mind. I thought back to the Van Gogh exhibit with Amanda, and her insistence that I notice the *Road Less Traveled* painting that day. Also, she couldn't seem to get enough of the *Sunflower* series.

The *Sunflower* series . . . Sunflower Street.

A coincidence, too? I thought not.

Finally, after a good twenty minutes of pedaling, the situation was starting to look a bit more promising. The tall, haylike grass that bordered our path was beginning to thin out. We also passed by a couple of ranches with spotlights shining over them, as if people were actually living there. Callie suggested we might stop at one of them to use their phone, since none of our cells were working out here, but Zoe and Hal insisted that they were starting to recognize things.

"I could've sworn we passed by that house on the way out here," he said, pointing to a cabin in the distance.

I was pretty sure I'd seen it, too. It had white accents, a large front porch, and was positioned beside what appeared to be a storage facility of some sort.

"I'm almost positive that we rode up on the other side of it," Hal said. "On the way to the hangar. The main road must be on the other side."

"Kind of focused on pedaling here," Callie huffed, although actually, she was barely winded. "Tell me where to go, and I'll go."

Without a word, Hal continued to pedal, cutting through someone's backyard and passing by a strip of abandoned cars, until we finally reached the back of the cabin.

The street was visible through the driveway.

"Yes!" Zoe pumped her fist.

"Remain seated until the captain has turned off the seat belt sign," Callie snapped. "No sudden movement."

We rode through the owner's driveway, and finally back out onto the road. It was all I could do to contain myself from cheering—that's how relieved I was. How relieved we *all* were.

Zoe hopped off Callie's handlebars. "We're free!" she shouted, rubbing at the literal pain in her butt from Callie's handlebars.

We all spent the next several minutes calling our parents and coming up with some creative excuses about where we'd been all day.

"We just got out of the Bogart festival," I told my mother, feeling a lot less guilty for lying, considering that she was keeping secrets, too. "We were all going to head over to school now for the talent show . . . if that's okay?"

My mother hesitated a moment. "I made us some cinnamon *churros*; I thought we might sit and chat for a while before I have to head down to the church for the final auction setup."

"Oh, sorry," I said, my guilt returning.

"But you go with your friends," she continued. "I'm glad you're having fun. We will have a very late dinner tonight. But if it gets too late, we won't wait. You can eat some leftovers when you get home and we can catch up then."

"Perfect, Mama." I smiled, flipping my phone shut. I peered down both ends of the street, suddenly—and almost surprisingly—invigorated about the idea of going to the talent show and hearing Hal play.

And getting to see West again.

CHAPTER 29

As we rode to the talent show, one of the clues we'd discussed kept nagging at me, pestering me, as if there were something we weren't quite seeing. The hospital bracelet. What were we overlooking about it?

"Take this left," Zoe called out, still helping to navigate our way back to the school from her perch on Callie's handlebars.

We turned the corner as she suggested, and I vaguely remembered Amanda once reminiscing about a friend of hers from childhood, from a town where she used to live. Could that have been Zoe?

"We used to have so much fun together," Amanda said, after a poetry reading at the town library (the topic was journeys). "We'd make up our faces and put on old theater costumes. We'd take each other's pictures, and then go trick-or-treating around the neighborhood, even when it wasn't Halloween."

"That's certifiable, obviously," I told her, checking out some of the poetry selections on display.

"Maybe certifiable, but it still worked. We still collected candy, not to mention a lot of senior citizens' smiles. I really miss living in that town." Her face grew suddenly pensive, but she tried to cover it up by pointing to one of the poem's messages: "But I suppose the only journey worthwhile is the one that moves forward, right?" she asked.

"We're here," Hal called with relief, a good fifteen minutes later, bringing me back to the present.

Still on our *own* journey, we rode around to the back parking lot. Meanwhile, the hospital bracelet clue plagued me, and it refused to let me go.

"I'm going to run ahead," Hal panted, leaping off the bike. "I asked my mom to bring my guitar over with some clothes early. Maybe I will have time to grab a shower in the gym and not have the lingering smell of moldy basement all over me. Wish me luck!" He ran ahead. We picked up his bike and walked with it through the parking lot.

Zoe also announced she was running ahead. "I'm helping the musicians with some of the warm-up—if that's okay with you guys."

"Go, go," I said, waving her off. "We have this covered."

"Well, look who's here." Callie pointed to West's Alfa Romeo. It was parked five cars in. "I say we check it out; there might be a clue hidden somewhere—under a headlight, or by the door handle maybe?"

It was definitely worth a look. And so we circled the perimeter of the car a couple times before Callie finally spotted the message.

"Here," she said, pointing to the back bumper. It was a sticker that read IF YOU'RE FOLLOWING ME, YOU'RE ON THE RIGHT TRACK. In the bottom corner was a comic book–style drawing of a coyote, Amanda's totem.

That bumper was pristine when I saw the car the last time. Callie gave me a little fist bump, which I tentatively returned.

It felt almost exhilarating. Because we *were* on the right track. And I felt like we were closer than ever.

We were heading to the school when I took a step back. "I can't," I told her.

"What's wrong?" Callie asked, reaching out to touch my shoulder.

I drew a deep breath, knowing that no matter how hard I tried to squelch it, I couldn't ignore my gut: "I have to go check on something," I told her. "And I have to do it now. Go on in. I'll be back in a little while."

"What do you have to check? And it has to be this minute?" Callie asked.

"If I go now, I'll be back soon and won't miss

anything. There isn't time to explain."

"Go," Callie said. Her mouth formed a straight tense line, as if she completely understood that sometimes these things are bigger than we are.

"I'll only be a half hour behind you guys," I insisted. "Five minutes to get home; five minutes to get back. I won't miss Hal's act." I glanced down at my watch. There was still a half hour left before the show even started.

Callie gave me a hug and wished me luck, then took the remaining bikes to lock them up.

I got back on my bike, raced home, and bolted up the stairs two at a time. The smell of cinnamon *churros* was thick in the air, but my mother was already gone. No doubt she'd left for church shortly after my phone call. My father wasn't home either (likely working late), and I knew that Cisco was already at the talent show. He'd been keeping his participation a secret for fear that our dad would've tried to talk him out of it, reminding him of his priorities; i.e, to try to keep his energy focused on his "soccer stardom."

Cisco had prepared a monologue from *A Midsummer Night's Dream*. Dressed as Puck in a long tank and a crown of leaves, he'd practiced his act in front of me a couple of times, and I had to admit, it was breathtaking.

In my room, I pulled Amanda's box from the back of my closet and took out the hospital bracelet. I looked at the date, February 13, knowing that Amanda and I had been together that day.

t was a Sunday night, and we were sitting at the sushi bar of Asahi, the Japanese restaurant down the street from Endeavor.

"I adore this place," Amanda said, watching the sushi chefs roll maki behind the glass.

It was a little odd being there, just the two of us, mostly because it was the eve of Valentine's Day, and the place was filled with happy couples looking to celebrate before the work week started up. Normally, we'd have headed to Taco King or Pizza Luigi's, but Amanda thought it would be a celebration to reward ourselves.

"Just think about the money we saved today," she said, reminding me that the admission to the literature fest we'd just attended was $25 a ticket. But she'd won free passes at a library raffle. "We deserve a little maki indulgence, don't you think?"

It sounded like a good enough idea, but that was before I noticed all the lovestruck couples and the heart-shaped votive candle on the bar in front of us.

"You know what I think?" Amanda said, ordering us a couple cups of green tea. "This is the perfect day for a celebration."

"Well, it is practically Valentine's Day." I nodded toward an overly cozy couple just behind us.

"That's not what I mean." She looked deliberately at me, not at them. "Don't let some incidental date on the calendar dictate our celebration. Why can't we just relish the day, the fact that we're alive, enjoying each other's company, and trying new food?"

"Because it's Valentine's Day," I joked.

"Valentine's Eve," she corrected me.

"Which is still the holiday for lovers. And I suppose we have Chaucer to thank for that."

"Chaucer?" Amanda raised an eyebrow.

"It's true," I told her, reveling in the historical facts as usual. "Okay, so, yes, February fourteenth is known for the patron saint who refused to give up his religion after he married people on the sly and was thus executed for it. But Chaucer was the one who really linked the day to love."

Amanda clasped her hand over her mouth, as if something really tragic had happened. "How did I not know this?"

I leaned forward eagerly, thrilled to share. "During medieval times, some believed that birds mated on February fourteenth."

"Which makes complete sense"—Amanda lit up—"because Chaucer uses birds as a symbol of love in his poetry."

"Fascinating, right?"

A second later the waiter came and delivered our tea, asking if we wanted to hear about the love specials. Apparently everyone's sushi orders were being arranged in heart shapes.

"No thank you," Amanda told him. She turned to me, once the waiter was out of earshot. "Mark it on your calendar. February thirteenth, a day to celebrate life. Even Chaucer wouldn't disagree."

"Chaucer's dead."

"But obviously his words live on." Amanda held up her cup of steaming green tea.

I raised my cup to toast with hers, and we ended up treating the rest of our dinner like a holiday, even ordering celebratory cake at the end, along with glasses of faux-champagne.

I looked back down at the hospital bracelet, confident now that February 13, that day at the sushi bar, had indeed been her birthday. That had to be what we were celebrating. "Ariel Feckerol," I whispered, suddenly noticing that some of the lettering on the bracelet had worn off.

I grabbed a pen and filled in the missing segments, turning Feckerol into Beckendorf with just a few quick strokes. But still, as exciting as it felt to figure out just one more piece, it was frustrating not to be able to envision anything when I touched the bracelet—when I rubbed my thumb over her name, wore it on my finger, or held it up to my forehead.

I picked through some of the other items inside the box, determined to find something—anything—that would make this pit stop more worthwhile. I raked through a plethora of photographs, concentrated hard on a bag of sand, and flipped through a whole stack of postcards.

But there was nothing.

I felt nothing.

And I envisioned even less.

I took a deep breath, wondering why this power was so erratic—why one minute I'd touch something and the vision would be so distinct.

And then something like this would happen.

I wondered if it had something to do with Hal, Callie, and Zoe. It seemed some of the most significant visions I'd gotten happened when I was in their presence. Or in the presence of at least one of them.

I shoved the photos back inside the box, along with the postcards and the bag of sand. I was just about to close everything up when something caught my eye.

On the underside of the box's lid there was a bulge beneath the velvet lining.

I ran my fingers over it, feeling a soft lump. Something was hidden inside. I tugged at a corner of the lining, noticing how the stitching wasn't consistent all the way around. It was tight along three sides of the lid but much looser at the bottom, as if that side had been restitched by hand.

Without hesitation, I tore at the stitches and ripped open the seams. Within seconds, one side was completely open. I stuck my fingers in; my middle finger brushed against something soft.

I plucked it out. It was a swatch of pink fabric, no bigger than the palm of my hand. One side was fuzzy, while the other had a silky feel. I was almost positive it was from a baby blanket. The edges were frayed where the swatch had been cut from the larger whole. I flipped it onto the silky side, noticing a couple of embroidered letters: an A with half of a lowercase R.

"Ariel," I whispered, knowing that this had been a section of her baby blanket—Amanda's baby blanket.

I smoothed my palm over the fuzzy side, able to picture clearly the entire scene: baby Ariel sleeping peacefully in her crib; a moon-and-stars mobile hovering just above her, with the ARIEL blanket covering her middle. I pressed my eyes shut and could see the loopy lettering of her name. It had been done with a sparkly gold embroidery thread, appearing brighter and cheerier than its current drab state. And her birth date, February 13, had been stitched just below it. I concentrated harder, noticing how a corner of the blanket had been folded downward, stuck under baby Ariel's chubby little leg.

I opened my eyes, continuing to palm the fabric, spotting a bit of yellow embroidery by the torn side, no bigger than the size of my thumb. Was that the part that'd been stuck under the baby's leg? I ran my hand over it, wondering what it could have been. A design of some sort? More lettering, or an essential clue?

Beyond anxious to get back to the others, I stuffed the blanket swatch into my pocket, crammed everything else back inside my closet, and hurried out the door.

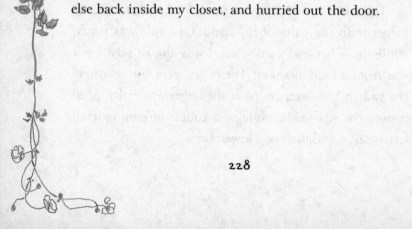

CHAPTER 30

I burst through the doors of the gym building, but Mrs. Watson stopped me just short of the auditorium.

"Ticket, please," she said.

"Really?" I asked, all out of breath.

"Do I look like I'm joking?"

It was actually hard to judge, considering the clown wig and muumuu dress she was wearing (complete with equations and formulas patterned on the fabric and the sequined number earrings). I assumed the get-up was for the occasion, but on second thought, I couldn't be sure.

"Ten dollars per ticket," she said. "Tonight's a fundraiser, remember?"

"Right," I said, fishing a couple of rolled-up fives from my wallet.

Mrs. Watson stamped my wrist with a smiley face,

handed me a voting ballot, and I was in—just in the nick of time to catch Heidi and her dancing clonettes. They were lip-synching to "It's Raining Men," a 1980s song. Heidi, Kelli, Traci, and Lexi held matching umbrellas to protect themselves from the storm of naked Ken dolls that poured down from the ceiling.

Classy.

The auditorium was packed, and not just with students and chaperones. Parents came, too—hordes of them—cheering on their sometimes dubiously talented offspring. Case in point: Chief Bragg was sitting in the front row, videotaping Heidi's whole lip-synch routine, even as a GI Joe doll bopped her on the head.

Finally, I spotted Callie and Zoe standing at the side, a bit back from the stage. Callie was uneasily watching for me, and Zoe was talking to some members of the glee club. Was there anyone that girl didn't know? I made my way over to them.

"Well?" Callie asked, anxious to hear what I'd found out.

"We'll discuss it later," I said, reluctant to get into it now. "Where's Hal?"

"Backstage, practicing." She gazed up at the I-Girls, and gave a subtle shake of her head, probably wondering how she ever could've been one of them.

Finally, once Heidi's act was over, Callie raved about Cisco—about how amazing his monologue was, and that he should really look into acting.

"So, I missed it?" I asked, dismayed. Fortunately I had seen it at home. I could fake my way through some congratulations.

"*So* good," Zoe continued, turning away from her glee club friends without missing a beat. "I mean, look-out-Hollywood. That boy definitely gets my vote." She flashed me her filled-in ballot with Cisco's name at the very top.

"Wait, what about Hal's band?" Callie pointed out.

"Right." Zoe nodded. "I probably need a few more ballots."

I rolled my eyes as the two of them turned all fangirl on me—as Zoe marveled about my brother's quote-unquote sexy eyes, and as Callie went into way too much detail describing his well-worked chest under the leafy tank he'd been wearing as Puck.

When I'd heard thoroughly enough about my brother's "hotness," West appeared on the stage and grabbed the microphone at the front, and with it my complete attention.

The band was arrayed behind him: Hal on guitar, Kofi Chamblee on the drums, and a kid named Charlie Miles playing keyboard.

West was dressed in dark vintage-looking jeans and a basic tee, and his hair was caught somewhere between slicked back and artfully messy—sort of a 1950s greaser look, set in the present day.

A second before the band started to play, West looked in my direction and did that shoot-you-with-a-finger move, before starting to hit the chords on his bass guitar.

And then he started to sing.

His voice was silky-smooth, reminding me a little of Frank Sinatra's or Harry Connick Jr.'s. I felt my body sway from side to side, completely swept up in the moment and in West's voice, and in the way he kept glancing toward me, as if checking that I was still there.

The band was spectacular. The way the members came together—their voices and instruments culminating into one truly amazing sound—it just brought the music to a whole new level.

Sort of like us, Amanda's guides.

When the song was over, Hal's parents, sitting in the front row with Cornelia, jumped out of their seats to give the band a standing ovation. Meanwhile, West came down from the stage.

And made a beeline for me.

"Hey." He smiled, standing right in front of me now. "I'm so glad you came."

"Yes, well, of course I came," I said.

"Yes, well, I'm glad." He smiled wider.

"You guys were incredible," I said, wanting to congratulate Hal as well, but he was surrounded by Cornelia and his parents.

Only a couple of seconds later, the next act began. It

was Tara Tate and Muriel Spencer, performing a peculiar good-versus-evil dance, equipped with pitchforks and angels' wings.

"Do you think that hurts?" West asked, after an unfortunate entanglement between the forks and the wings when the girls collided.

I couldn't help but laugh, which felt really good. Because I just hadn't laughed in a while.

Finally, Hal came and joined us, heading straight to Callie first. The two smiled at a private joke, and then Hal turned to me and asked me if I had any news.

I looked at West, hating to leave him but knowing that we had very pressing matters. "I'm really sorry," I told him, "but would you mind excusing us for a few minutes?"

"No problem," he said, still watching the show, but venturing to touch my forearm, which made my heart beat at quadruple its normal speed.

I led Hal, Callie, and Zoe into a corner by the coat rack and tried to convey my overpowering motivation: inspired by the lightning-bolt-like jolt that pulsed through my body upon joining hands in the barn, I wanted to try touching some of the items in Amanda's box.

"Did you picture anything?" Hal asked.

"In a way, but not in the exact way I'd hoped." I told them about Amanda's birthday at the sushi restaurant, and how I was obsessed with that hospital bracelet. "I felt like I needed to touch it—to see if I could picture anything."

"And did you?" Zoe asked.

I shook my head. "And so I just started touching everything in there, trying to justify my reason for going home in the first place. But I didn't envision anything."

"Until?" Hal asked, as if reading my mind.

"Until I discovered that the box had a secret compartment. It was under the lid. And there was something hidden in the lining." I pulled the swatch from my pocket, pointing out the capital A and the lowercase R.

"Why would this scrap be hidden?" Zoe asked, brushing her fingers over the fuzzy fabric.

"I don't know, but it's clearly from her baby blanket. I was able to picture the whole thing—the crib, the mobile, the nursery, even baby Ariel."

"Aka Baby Amanda," Callie breathed.

"Aka Ariel Feckerol." Hal sighed.

"You'll be pleased to learn that Feckerol is actually Beckendorf minus a few strokes, most likely attributable to wear, tear, and age," I told them.

"And that would make me pleased *because* . . . ?" he asked, looking cranky.

"Because it's one less name we need to worry about." I gave him an optimistic smile.

"All this baby stuff," Callie said. "I mean, do you think there's some significance to it all?"

"Well, Thornhill did say that Amanda's birth was definitely key," I reminded them.

At the same moment, Zoe pointed out the bit of yellow embroidery by the swatch's torn edge. "What's this?" she asked.

But before I could say anything, someone bumped into me from behind. I stumbled forward and then turned to look.

"Sorry about that," an unfamiliar woman said.

I managed a polite smile at her, as if it were no big deal. But that was before I noticed that she was carrying the same pink vintage clutch purse that Waverly Valentino had when she came to my house.

It was unmistakable.

"What's wrong?" Hal asked, following my gaze.

The woman, in a halter dress and suede cowboy boots, had skin the color of hot cocoa and big violet eyes that matched the color of her coat. "The clutch," I said.

"What clutch?" Zoe took a step forward, trying to get a better look, but it was getting harder to maneuver. More people had crowded into the auditorium as we neared the show's finale. A long line of band members marched in front of us, blocking our view.

Hal appeared confused as well, but Callie knew. Her eyes zeroed in on the big, floppy flower attached to the front of the bag, as it bobbed and weaved—seemingly disembodied—through the crowd.

"You don't think it's the same one, do you?" she asked, practically shouting now. Members of a marching band were tooting their horns—literally—as they threaded their way through the crowd toward the center aisle. Meanwhile, the woman got farther away, almost to the exit doors.

"We have to talk to her," Callie insisted.

Before we could even get close, a squad of cheerleaders intercepted us with an impromptu dance-cheer. Callie did her best to skirt around them, even taking a pom-pom in the face, but we still ended up getting stopped at the door. A few members of the talent show committee were insisting that we turn in our voting ballots before we left the show.

Finally out in the lobby, the woman was nowhere to be found.

"Where did she go?" Callie asked, rubbing at her eye.

We looked all around, finally spotting the woman on her cell phone, just steps from the main door.

"Excuse me, ma'am?" Callie called out to her.

The woman turned in our direction. "Can I help you?" she asked, flipping her phone shut. There was a Southern drawl to her voice.

She couldn't have been more than twenty-five, with pretty cornrows swept back in a half ponytail, and earrings that dangled to her shoulders.

"That bag," I said, nodding toward it.

"Like it?" She beamed. "I just bought it at a second-hand shop downtown."

"Which shop?" I asked.

The woman pondered a couple seconds, her eyes rolled up toward the ceiling, as if trying her best to remember. "Sam's Place . . . or Play It, Sam . . . something like that."

"Play It Again, Sam's," I whispered, suddenly remembering how Louise had said an interesting character had come into her shop to buy and then return something. I bet that person was Waverly Valentino. Of course, the *why* was still an issue.

"It was only my first time in there," the woman continued. "You all should check it out . . . some pretty nice stuff."

"When did you get it?" Callie asked.

"Just yesterday." She wedged the clutch up under her arm, as if to pose. A wide smile spread across her face.

"I want to buy it," I said. Callie and Zoe looked shocked at my boldness.

Her smile faded. "You *can't* buy it. This is a one-of-a-kind. The saleslady assured me of it. You won't see this one coming and going."

"You don't understand," I said, pulling my wallet from my bag. "I want to buy this one . . . from you."

Realizing I would not be stopped, Callie tried, too. "Please," she begged, taking out her wallet as well. "That bag belonged to a friend of ours."

"We *think*," I said. "Or at least someone connected to our friend."

"It's sort of a long story," Callie explained. "But our friend is missing, and it'd mean a lot to us if you'd please—".

"Name your price," Hal said, finally catching up and pulling a couple of bunched-up tens from his pocket.

The woman's face grew puzzled as we all pooled our money together. "Well, I don't know," she said, seemingly unnerved. A tiny frown formed on her rosebud lips.

"Please." Zoe's voice was calm but resolute. It seemed to do the trick.

"Well . . . ," she said, giving the bag a once-over. "I suppose since it means so much to you . . . How about forty-five dollars? That's what the purse cost me."

Forty-five dollars: exactly $7.75 shy of what we actually had.

"It's fine," the woman said, taking all of our money, but forgoing Hal's random offer of a Silly Putty egg that he had in his pocket.

"It's all I have left," he said with a shrug.

The woman emptied the contents of her purse into a shopping bag she was carrying. And in doing so, I saw it.

The purse's lining.

I spotted the lettering and the fuzzy pink material.

It was from Ariel's baby blanket.

CHAPTER 31

Once the woman had gone, Callie pulled the purse lining forward, having caught a glimpse of it as well. The remainder of a lowercase R was there, as were the rest of the letters: the I, the E, and the loopy lowercase L. Somehow the lettering was still recognizable despite all the wear and tear it had seen. It was covered with a layer of dirt, and it looked like some of the embroidery stitching had worn away. But even more fascinating was what we found at the very bottom of the purse, beneath a bubblegum wrapper.

An embroidered sunflower, missing just one petal.

Zoe took the blanket swatch from her pocket and pieced the sunflower together, using the shred of yellow embroidery by the swatch's torn edge. "Like two pieces of a vintage puzzle," she said.

"Like Sunflower Street," Hal reminded us.

"Not to mention a Van Gogh exhibit that Amanda and I once visited," I told them. "And the sunflower on Rantoul Street."

"Am I missing something? A what on where?" Hal asked, shaking his head.

"After we attempted to visit the pharmacy," I explained, "and you guys had already taken off for home, I saw a sunflower spray-painted on the side of the gas station building. You probably saw it"—I looked at Zoe— "you were hot on our trail."

"Seriously?" Hal asked. Zoe said nothing.

I nodded. "It took up half the side of the building."

"So what does it all mean?" Callie asked.

"Well, some say that the sunflower is a symbol for power," I began. "Because the sun is all-powerful, and the sunflower follows it around."

"My father used to tell us that story. From Greek mythology," Zoe said, clearly familiar with the legend.

"Exactly," I said. "Amanda and I used to dissect Greek myths. Basically the sun god Helios was beloved by a girl named Clytie who, as the legend states, died of her love for him. Some believe that she then became a sunflower, so that she could bask in his light."

"Meaning that we should bask in Amanda's light?" Zoe made a face.

"I'd go with the first theory," Hal said. "Maybe this has more to do with power. A power as strong as the sun."

"A power just like ours—together," I whispered.

"So, then we should follow it," Callie chimed in. "Follow *her*, I mean. Because we *are* on the right track."

"Still, I just don't get it," Hal said, looking toward the exit doors. "This whole scene . . . what just happened with the bag . . . it all seems a little too convenient for my taste. A little too perfect."

"You think it was more than coincidence?" Callie asked. "Like maybe we were *supposed* to see that woman? Maybe someone sent her here?"

"Someone like Amanda," I said, somewhat under my breath.

Instead of answering, Hal hurried to the exit doors. He tore them open, as if we'd just been duped.

"Where are you going?" Callie called out after him.

Hal took a few steps out into the traffic circle in front of the gym. I moved to the double glass doors to have a look as well, but it appeared as though the woman had already gone. A dark sedan pulled onto the main road and sped away with a screech.

"Who was she?" Hal asked, whipping the door open to join us back inside.

"I don't know," Callie said. "I've never seen her before."

"Did you see her talking to anyone?"

I shook my head, disappointed we hadn't asked her more questions.

"I think Hal's right," Zoe said, fidgeting with her

beaded bracelet. "The timing was just a wee bit too perfect."

"That woman was probably too young to be a parent," Callie said, thinking out loud. "And I didn't notice her cheering anyone on."

"Plus, I'm not quite sure I buy that, of all the people in the auditorium, she just happened to accidentally bump into Nia," Hal continued.

"Yes, but don't you think it'd be a long shot even for Amanda to assume I'd recognize a sunflower clutch?"

"Well, now that you mention it, you have been kind of an accessories maven lately," Callie said, eyeing my new alligator ring.

"It's all a long shot." Hal let out a frustrated sigh.

We remained in the lobby for several more seconds, until something drew us back into the auditorium.

Or, rather, some*one*.

Someone whose voice was as smooth and melodic as trickling water. And suddenly we were like rats to the Pied Piper's tune. We headed to the auditorium doorway, eager to find the source.

It was Bea. She was the last act of the night, singing the song she'd chosen—or, more correctly, the song that Amanda had chosen for her.

"'You've Got a Friend,'" Zoe burst out. "James Taylor . . . I love this song."

And now, listening to Bea, and feeling the warmth of her voice as it washed over my skin, I loved it, too.

People in the audience rocked back and forth. Best friends hugged. Strangers teared up. People cheered. And Hal reached down to take Callie's hand.

"She's really talented," Zoe whispered.

At the close of her song, Bea got a standing ovation. And it came as no surprise to anyone when several minutes later, after counting up all the ballots (we rushed to vote again), Mrs. Bragg, the parent-chairperson of the talent show, got up and reluctantly announced that Bea was the winner.

What *did* come as a surprise was that Mrs. Bragg was able to stand up there with a completely straight face and announce that Heidi had come in second.

And that wasn't her only surprising announcement.

"I'm delighted to say that the history club has a few more spots left open for its trip to Washington, D.C., next week," she said. "It's very last-minute, so if anyone is interested, please let Mr. Fowler know."

"We need to go on that," Callie said, giving Hal's hand an extra squeeze. She passed me the clutch bag, and then she and Hal moved farther inside the doorway, perhaps to get more information.

I opened the bag and felt the liner inside. At the same moment, an icy sensation bit at my skin, nearly bringing me to my knees.

"What is it?" Zoe asked, grabbing me by the arm, as if I might collapse at any moment.

A poisonous taste filled my mouth and I wanted to

be sick. I closed my eyes, trying to will the image away. I shook my head, took several steps back, and even covered my ears.

"What is it?" Zoe demanded again; her voice had an echoing quality that reverberated in my brain.

When I didn't answer, she led me to a bench outside, sat me down, and patted my back. "You can tell me," she insisted. "You've got a friend, remember?"

I looked down at the blanket liner, still clenched in my hands, wadded up in the sweat of my palms. My head was spinning. And my mouth tasted like it was filled with foam.

"Death," I managed to whisper. "I can see it everywhere."

"What do you mean *you can see it?*" she asked. "Does it have a face? Do you picture something specific? Are you talking about . . . Amanda?" Her voice trembled over that last question.

"I can see it," I repeated, touching the fabric harder. In doing so, the images in my mind became clearer: blue lights flashing, blood against cobblestone, a casket lowered down into the ground, a sea of black clothing, and a field of red poppies.

"Nia?" Zoe asked. She continued to rub my back.

"It isn't Amanda." I shook my head. Tears formed at the rims of my eyes. I released my grip on the fabric, but for some reason it didn't help. "It's death from the past,"

I told her. "I'm sure of it."

"*How* are you sure?"

"I just am," I said, a constricting sensation inside my throat. "Everything I picture is from the past."

"Well, then whose death do you see?"

I met her eyes finally. The images still floated across my mind, almost blocking my ability to see her completely. "I'm not sure." I ventured to look away—at Callie and Hal, lingering in the doorway of the auditorium, completely unaware of what just happened.

Of what I could see.

Of what I was *still* seeing.

I closed my eyes, hoping that would help—that it would make the images go away.

It didn't.

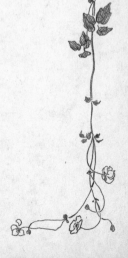

A BIG ROUND OF THANKS

I could not have recounted my story in such detail without the help of everyone on the site. You are my eyes and ears, and do not think that any observation, no matter how small, ever went unnoticed.

Herewith, an index of your amazing contributions.

—Nia

MANY THANKS TO:

HOW I MET AMANDA

Hi everyone—I just wanted to share the story of how I met Amanda:

It was winter. One of those "middle" days of January—the 13th or 14th or 15th—that usually all blur together in a big rainy mess. However, this day was a day I would never forget. I was sitting on the back steps of the art department, listening to the sharp metallic "tap" of the rain on the roof and watching the water pool up on the ground. Pool up and then spill over, leaving little moist streams on the asphalt.

I sighed and lay my head back on the side of the building. My brother was late to pick me up, as usual. He was what my mother liked to call a "free spirit." I just thought he was a slacker. I had a calculus test the next day, and I was almost too involved in running integrals and derivatives through my head to look up when I heard a voice on the pathway in front of me.

It was a girl, singing. She had a beautiful voice. It

didn't seem like she was singing one song in particular, but rather bits and pieces of things that I knew I had heard before but couldn't quite place. She came towards me, walking in a graceful way that almost seemed more like dancing. She was staring up at the sky, smiling at the raindrops that were plummeting down to earth. Unlike all of the other frantic students who had rushed by, holding up umbrellas to "protect" themselves from the rain and loudly complaining about their wet hair, this girl seemed unperturbed and in no hurry whatsoever.

In fact, she seemed so peaceful and introspective that I almost thought she would walk right past me without a word. However, as she got closer, she started talking. I was confused at first, as she still wasn't looking at me.

"Hi," she said. "I'm Amanda."

"Hi," I said warily, staring somewhat rudely at her brown hair, which that week she had embellished with pink streaks.

"I know you," she said. "You're Stefanie." She suddenly plopped onto the stoop next to me, smoothing out her polka-dot skirt once she was settled.

"Yep," I said tersely. I wasn't trying to be rude, but I was already upset with my brother and honestly, she did look a little strange.

"It's okay," she said, as if reading my thoughts. "I won't bother you for long. I just wanted to say hello."

Suddenly, I felt guilty. Even though she didn't seem

upset, I still felt like I should compensate for my behavior in some way.

"That's okay," I said, turning towards her and smiling. "I don't have anything important to be doing anyways."

"Everything's important," she said, suddenly becoming serious. "Always remember that. Value your own time, value everything you do. One day, everything could just disappear."

We both stared at the rain for a minute. I was absorbing what she had just said, and she was smiling up at the rain.

"Anyways," she said, standing up. "It was delightful to meet you, Stefanie. I hope to see you again."

I hoped so, too.

—Stef Stone

About the Author: Olivia Moore is a high school senior in Oregon, and hopes to be a writer one day. In her free time she enjoys playing tennis, writing for her school newspaper, and spending time with her labradoodle, Micalene. She loves reading, and the Amanda Project is one of her favorite book series.

Member Since: April 13, 2009
She knows why Amanda came here, and thinks the best breakfast is a sesame bagel toasted with no cream cheese.

unraveled . . .

I may not have much in common with Nia, Callie, and Hal, but there is one thing we share, aside from the fact that we are in danger. What links us is that we all divide our existence at Endeavor High into two parts: Before Amanda. And After.

When Amanda came to our school, she made me feel like I could tell her anything, that she saw the good, the bad, and the ugly inside me. Sure, Amanda called me on the lies I tell myself, but she also made me feel honest and strong.

Amanda did all of this for me. The first time was when we were eight and her parents and my parents were friends.

The second time was last fall.

Both times, just as I was getting used to having her around, she disappeared.

Friends, It's Zoe. I know you don't know me, especially the way you know Hal, Callie, and Nia. But I've been watching, since the beginning. I'm writing the final chapter in Amanda's story, and I promise you, everything is coming to light.

This is it. The end of it all. Or maybe, as Amanda would say, the beginning.

You'll have to read *Unraveled* to find out. . . .

Until then, see you on the site.

—Zoe

Laurie Faria Stolarz is the author of several popular young adult novels, including *Deadly Little Secret*, *Deadly Little Lies*, *Deadly Little Games*, *Project 17*, *Bleed*, and the bestselling Blue Is for Nightmares series. Stolarz's titles have been part of the Quick Pick for Reluctant Readers list, the Top Ten Teen Pick list, and YALSA's Popular Paperback list, all through the American Library Association. Born and raised in Salem, Massachusetts, Stolarz attended Merrimack College and received an MFA in creative writing from Emerson College in Boston. For more information, visit Laurie's website at www.lauriestolarz.com.

This is the story of Amanda Valentino. She makes things happen for her own reasons.

For exclusive information on your
favorite authors and artists, visit
www.authortracker.com.

CORNELIA'S CODE

Hey, Guys!

Cornelia here. Have you ever seen someone and wondered if they know what you know? Or wondered how to let them know that you know that they know what you know, without actually saying it, just in case they don't know what you know? Luckily, I've come up with the perfect solution—datamatrix codes! They're BIG in Japan, which means they're headed this way. (Um, Pokémon? Sushi? Hello Kitty? Need I say more?)

I looove using new technology (duh), which is why I am SO excited for you guys to start using the codes to help Hal, Callie, and Nia find Amanda.

Basically, a datamatrix code is a bar code like the ones you're used to seeing in stores . . . only way cooler. You don't need a special scanner, just a phone with camera and internet connection. To read them, all you have to do is:

- Use your phone to download the 2D Bar Code reader software at http://theamandaproject.mobi/thereader
- Fire it up (it's usually under Applications)
- Snap a picture of the code using your phone's camera

And voilà! The browser on your phone will automatically unlock the magic programmed into the code—a secret website with video, messages, pictures, and more!

So, what's the secret in this code? You'll have to scan to find out. And remember— the next time you see a code it might be a message from me, or from Amanda, or from that new girl at school who wants to know if you know what she knows . . .

Over and out
— Cornelia B.

Who is AMANDA VALENTINO?

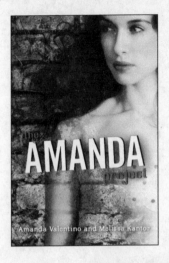

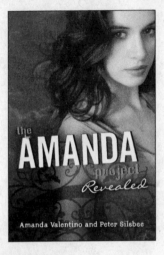

And don't miss the fourth book
in the series . . . UNRAVELED.

Help write Amanda's story at www.theamandaproject.com.